PRAISE FO

MW00488652

'A beautifully crafted and immersing novel asking uneasy and provocative questions that insist on responses.'
— **Jenny Crwys-Williams**, Shortlist for *Fiction Book of the Year 2015*

'This is local writer Craig Higginson at the top of his game in a novel that is powerfully original and startling. Higginson's writing is polished and sparingly beautiful ... He also has a tight grip on the interiority of the characters who people this remarkable novel. We are left scoured by the depths people will plumb in their grasp at understanding their lives.'
— *Pretoria News*

'The beautifully poetic narrative is filled with sad imagery as gloomy mists creep from the pages into the reader's mind.'
— *Cult Noise*

'Craig Higginson somehow manages to balance the unrest of the past, the toll of the present and the uncertainty of the future ... It is unputdownable ... A nuanced literary investigation of the dream houses we build, be they physical or psychological. But dream houses are ethereal, transient and illusory. It is what they signify that must be answered for and few authors convey this better than Higginson.'
— *The Sunday Independent*

'Craig Higginson is in the vanguard of the latest and most exciting novelists in South Africa, both robust and sensitive, offering a barometer of the best to be expected from the newest wave of writing in the country.'
— **André Brink**

'*The Dream House* is an open and frank exploration of human life that resonates beyond race. Looksmart is a welcome new kind of character in the constantly evolving reality of African literature.'
— **Nadine Gordimer**

'*The Dream House* is beautifully written. Its politics is understated and its portrayal of South Africa is characterised by a constant movement between affection, anger, nostalgia, resistance and the characters' acceptance of what is part of the human condition.'
— **Mark Behr**

ALSO BY CRAIG HIGGINSON

The Landscape Painter (2011)

'It is in *The Landscape Painter* that Higginson unfolds the mastery of his craft on all fronts …
Haunting long after the last page is turned, *The Landscape Painter* is one of those rare gems
which allows readers to rediscover themselves. Higginson is already one of the finest
South African writers around, but his star is surely and steadily on the rise.'
— **Karina Brink,** *Sunday Independent*

'This is a deeply moving novel made up of contrasts and differences and difficulties and
oppositions that somehow, magically, render a unified and rewarding vision that haunts one
long after the final page is read. It is the result of sensitive craftsmanship and a palpable love
of story.'
— **Karen Scherzinger, University of Johannesburg Literary Awards 2012**

Last Summer (2010)

'In *Last Summer* the elegies of love are sung in measured and ironic tones. Higginson's narrative
poise, his understated and restrained emotional charge, are like cool air in our hot literary
landscape.'
— **Leon de Kock**

'The interest is altogether in the telling, in the delicacy and precision of the writing, and in
the subtle fluctuations between people that determine the outcomes of relationships and the
courses of lives … devastating …'
— **Michiel Heyns,** *Sunday Independent*

The Dream House

Craig Higginson

With 'The First Dream House' added for this edition

PICADOR AFRICA

First published in 2015 by Picador Africa, an imprint of Pan Macmillan South Africa

This edition published in 2016
by Picador Africa
Private Bag X19
Northlands
Johannesburg
2116

www.panmacmillan.co.za

ISBN 978-1-77010-489-1
e-ISBN 978-1-77010-490-7

© 2016, 2015 Craig Higginson

All rights reserved. No part of this publication may be reproduced, stored in or
introduced into a retrieval system, or transmitted, in any form, or by any means (electronic,
mechanical, photocopying, recording or otherwise) without the prior written permission of
he publisher. Any person who does any unauthorised act in relation to this publication
may be liable to criminal prosecution and civil claims for damages.

This book is a work of fiction. Any resemblance to actual places or persons, living or dead, is purely coincidental.

Editing by Alison Lowry
Proofreading by Sally Hines
Design and typesetting by Triple M Design, Johannesburg
Cover design by K4
Cover photograph by Craig Higginson

Printed and bound by

There is no better way to know us
Than as two wolves, come separately to a wood.
—TED HUGHES

The First Dream House

There are many houses we pass through during our lives. Maybe it's true that they also pass through us. Some of them remain with us, and we are able to return to them long after they are gone. One such house was a farmhouse in KwaZulu-Natal, just over the hill of the boarding school I attended between the ages of ten and fourteen. This hill stood above our school like the promise of another world. It provided the title for a novel of mine – simply called *The Hill* – and it now lies buried under a pine plantation. Where the air was once filled with the song of stonechats, longclaws and sunbirds, there is now only silence.

I came to know this house over the hill because on that farm were horses and my family was involved with horses. I forget the details, but I think my mother wanted to buy a horse from them – a Welsh pony, in fact – and we met them just as I was about to start at boarding school. We spent the night in that house and the next day I put on the strange new clothes for my school – a grey blazer and shorts, a black-and-white striped tie, a cap with the school logo sewn onto it and military tan shoes.

The farmer was a man from Yorkshire originally. He had a strong impenetrable accent, pale blue eyes and was always making jokes that insinuated themselves just around the borders of my comprehension. He was forever hinting at something sexual, it seemed to me, and I tended to smile at him whenever he looked in my direction – hoping to reassure him that I was quite fine as I was and that he needn't bother himself with me further.

It was the farmer's wife we were more concerned with – on that first meeting and afterwards. Even then she was a very large woman. She had a mop of frizzy greying hair, yellow teeth like bits of sweetcorn and laughing half-hidden eyes. She was also always making jokes, usually teasing me and my sister for being spoiled city kids. Actually, we lived in a very modest suburb in a very modest house, but to her we were shy, obscurely fastidious, possibly fussy children. We liked horses and dogs – and on that farm there were plenty of each – but we had never been in such a house, where the corners of every room hadn't been entered into in decades, and where everything smelt of old leather and wet wood and leaking gas.

I am not sure that the house made much impression on me at first as there was so much going on inside it and I must have been worried about going to a new school, but the farmer's wife said I should come and visit them on my first Sunday out. I could come for lunch and learn how to catch a fish. I dreaded the thought of this, but no one was going to take no for an answer and my mother was probably grateful there would be someone to pick me up – on a day when many of the other boys were being picked up by muddy bakkies from the neighbouring farms where they had grown up.

On the day in question, the farmer's wife was there to meet me outside the school library. She was in a large cream Mercedes and even then the car was being driven by a driver – Bheki – who wore neat blue overalls and never said a word. I sat in the back between two Alsatians. She sat in the passenger seat with at least three Chihuahuas on her lap. She chattered all the way through the woods and the dark thin road that led out the school, and didn't stop until we'd reached a dingy little shop run by an Indian man by the railway, where she gave me a few coins to go inside and buy myself some sweets. I did so, while they all waited in the car, and came back outside with my strange selection of toffees and 'nigger balls' and other little fruity sweets in a brown paper packet, immediately feeling that the day wouldn't be wholly bad after all.

I was in a daze for much of the time in those days and was probably far off and polite and eager to get my answers right. I was taken down the long dirt road that led to the farm, got out – large dogs sniffing my crotch, licking my hands, pawing at me with their mud – and joined her for tea and cake on the stoep. This ran along the front of the house, which had a shallow corrugated iron roof and resembled Karen Blixen's house in the film version of *Out of Africa*, in spite of being more modest and shabbier and perhaps not quite as old. That day I went fishing with Bheki and he hooked the fish and I ran with it up the bank – exactly as it was described in this book. The only difference is that the fish was a bass, not a rainbow trout, and we did indeed kill it. There is a photograph of me wearing the clothes of some other boy who once visited their house: a red T-shirt and tight blue shorts, holding up what was in effect another man's fish. My hair is brushed and I am standing upright, as if proud, although what I really felt at that moment is lost to me. I tend to look sceptical in photographs.

That was the first of many such visits. In time, I would come in the afternoons – usually with a friend or two – and we would drink Coke and eat some chocolate cake and get back to school just in time for showers. The house was a secret, a bolt hole that no teacher at the school knew about. It was my home away from home and I loved every bit of it and the farm around it. On my weekends out, I would often spend the night – staring at the high ceiling of the spare room while outside dogs barked and eagle-owls hooted and the rain smacked against the window. I continued to fish with mixed success and started to explore the surrounding hills – where I found a cave by a stream, a waterfall and the nests of malachite sunbirds, cape eagle-owls and crowned eagles. I could be happy for the day simply because I had spotted a rare kingfisher.

I think my imagination found a home during those years. When I started writing for the first time, it was in that spare room at a little desk, lit by a hurricane lamp. When I was working as the assistant to the theatre director Barney Simon, he encouraged me to start writing a play and the play took place in that house. This would eventually become my first original play, *Dream of the Dog* – later revisited and extensively developed as *The Dream House*. I have farmers in my family but grew up in a bland little suburb in Johannesburg – so this place provided me with magic, with a more abundant life. In those days, I wanted to be a vet. I would read books about horse ailments, I would watch cows and sheep and horses coupling and giving birth. I knew the house as a cool cave on hot summer days, as a rattling tin drum during thunderstorms, as a place of damp linen and crackling fireplaces when the mist filled the valley and seemed to invade every cupboard of the house. My time there opened my heart to such writers as William Wordsworth and Ted Hughes – so that when I arrived at their great poems I knew exactly what they were talking about.

I think the people who invited me into their home would be faintly horrified by what I've made of them. The farmer's wife would be amazed that Janet Suzman played her on London's West End. They had no idea there was anything artistic about me. If they had known, they would have laughed at it. They have long ago passed into the darkness we have all come from – and these days it sometimes feels as if I simply imagined them. They were people of their time, increasingly uneasy in a world that was rapidly outstripping them. But they were kind to me. Most of all, they left me alone. They provided a starting place for my imagination – as modest and meek as it might have been – to produce a little root, take hold and quietly nose its way towards the light.

Notes:

1. A version of this piece first appeared in the October–November 2015 edition of Visi, the architecture magazine.

2. I recently came across the couples' graves in a small churchyard near Nottingham Road. The teacher who inspired Mr Ford was also buried there. It was very strange to see the people who inspired three of my characters lying together there. I had made them love each other and hate each other in a way they never had in real life. Their real lives were already far off – and wholly unreachable.

One

Patricia

She draws back the curtains to reveal the mist. It has filled the whole valley and invaded every cupboard of the house. Her bedroom overlooks a row of kennels, silvery grey and subsiding at odd angles under a great green wave of brambles. The bloodwoods, solemn as totems, are barely visible above the old dog-run. She doesn't know what possessed them to plant those trees. To protect them from the wind, the sun, the view? It hardly matters now. Soon the trees will be cut down and cleared away, along with everything else. The people who come to live here afterwards will know nothing about any of them, and maybe it will be better that way.

All that Patricia has told him is that they are going away for a while. It doesn't make much sense. They have sold off all the livestock and equipment and packed the little they want to keep into boxes. Already the developers have moved in, reducing the stables and farm buildings to rubble, making fresh orange gashes across the fields to where the new houses will be, reducing the driveway — which went on for a kilometre through their valley — to a muddy bog. But Richard rarely leaves the house these days and nothing makes much sense to him anyway. To his queries about the recent packing up, all she has told him is that they are going away to the sea.

'Beauty?'

She can hear Beauty's footsteps progressing along the corridor: swift but provisional, expecting fresh instructions. Beauty will be on her way to dress Richard, the oats will have been cooked, the coffee brewed and the kitchen windows will be busy with the previous day's flies. Patricia knows every moment and mood of the house as intimately as she knows her own body. Better, in fact, as everything in the house can be reached for and grasped. Her body is an ageing and not quite trustworthy companion whose inner workings have only grown more mysterious over time.

'Beau-ty!'

Beauty will have heard her the first time, but she only ever responded on the second or third call, perhaps hoping Patricia would forget what she wanted, or forget that she wanted anything at all.

'Mesis?'

'Have you made the oats?'

'Yebo, Mesis.'

Beauty is wearing her blue overalls and a white doek, even though it's their last day. Her feet are bare, as usual. The rhythmic whisper of her feet up and down the corridor, like a conversation between two conspirators, once irritated Patricia, but these days she finds the sound comforting. In Durban, Beauty will go for driving and English lessons. She deserves a better job. Possibly as an au pair. Patricia and Richard will not be there forever and the girl will need to move on. She has a whole life ahead of her.

'I think we should have breakfast together today. Could you bring Richard through?'

'Yebo, Mesis.'

Patricia can see herself in the large mirror near the door. It was once attached to the wall and is speckled around the edges. There is a crack across the reflection of her throat. Her body is no longer able to fit into the mirror. It stands there like a pale floating lantern.

'This morning I have to go and see Mr Ford.'

'Yebo, Mesis. I will tell Bheki.'

'Thanks.'

Beauty crosses the room to fetch Patricia's walker – a battered metal frame that relieves some of the pressure off her back. The wheelchair, which lives in the sitting room, is something she tries to avoid: not only does it embarrass her, more recently it has started to dig into her back.

'I couldn't sleep last night. Could you?'

'Not so good, Mesis.'

'No, not so good at all.'

Outside, the old Rottweiler has started barking. Patricia always knows at once what the sound means: Ethunzini has seen one of the stable cats, a woman from the dairy is bringing in the morning milk, a stranger has arrived at the house, their car having survived the driveway. These days there is more traffic up and down their road, but it's usually earthmovers and trucks. Ethunzini, who hasn't quite worked out how to handle them, contents herself with barking from the apparent safety of the lawn.

This eruption means the morning milk, so they both ignore it.

Breakfast is laid out as usual in the small room at the back of the house, which adjoins the kitchen. The window panes are indeed being patrolled by flies. Through the mist, Patricia can see the fir tree outside where the bodies of freshly slaughtered lambs were hung. The two rows of bloodwoods that lead towards the dairy and the larger sheds march off in ever-diminishing tones of grey.

Rupert and George would normally have been there to greet her before returning to snapping up the flies, but she had them shot a week ago and buried under the fir tree at the front. Only Ethunzini remains. Although of the same dotage as the two Alsatians, Patricia hasn't yet had the stomach to have the Rottweiler killed. But her grave has been waiting for her all week, flanked by those of the Alsatians, as though the other two dogs, who were always more adventurous, have gone to secure the underworld ahead of her.

All her life, Patricia has been accompanied by a hurricane of dogs. Usually Chihuahuas and a Rottweiler, and a few variations between. The last Chihuahua – Finnegan – died in her lap eighteen months ago. Her heart just stopped. When her body had gone cold, Patricia asked Bheki to bury her in the bloodwood grove, where all the other dogs had been buried. It was on that day that she decided to sell the farm.

It was the right decision, of course. Even back then Richard needed a proper trained nurse. And it was ridiculous the way he sometimes wandered about. Shortly after the death of Finnegan, he disappeared for a whole night. Bheki later found him naked inside a disused porcupine hole that he'd scooped out. There were bits of grass and burrs in his beard. Patricia and Beauty had a private laugh about it, but it couldn't carry on. None of it could. She worked out that if she sold the farm, there would still be enough to live off.

The Durban house was a hundred and fifty years old and whenever anyone walked inside it, it creaked like an ancient ship. It stood on top of the hill in Glenwood and overlooked the harbour and the bluff. It was the house she had grown up in and she has had dreams about it her whole adult life. She wanted to spend her last days doing little more than staring at the sea.

She pours a glass of orange juice from the Toby jug and, grunting with the pain of it, sits. There are still weaver birds nesting in the fir tree. They sway and twitter and clack. The room smells of Alsatian and oats and leaking gas. She has decided not to get the cooker fixed: she has been rather hoping the whole house would go up in smoke, with all of them inside it.

'Eh?'

Even now Richard has the ability to appear by magic. He must have evaded Beauty as he's still wearing his pyjamas: pale blue cotton, stained with tea and smears of bran rusk. The pyjamas are the same steady tone as his gaze, which is fixed on Patricia as if she's an oncoming storm.

'Morning, Richard. Are you going to sit?'

'Eh?'

'Would you like a cup of tea? Beau-ty!'

'I want to take the dogs.'

'What?'

'To my father's place. I want to take them there tonight.'

'Right.'

It is not the fact of the dogs being shot that amuses her: it is that his father died twenty years ago.

'What's there to laugh about?' he wants to know.

'Your father is – no longer with us.'

'What are you talking about?'

'Too many pies.'

Richard turns away from this and sits. He stares at his hands.

'But I saw him only yesterday. We shared a cigarette.'

Beauty appears and goes over to the stove to revive the oats. Richard doesn't seem to notice her. Although he was never much of a farmer, he has the hands of one. How long has it been since Patricia last touched them? Or been touched by them? She probably comes into contact with them every day, but contact is very far from touch.

'Where's the television gone?'

'Packed.'

'Someone must have taken it.'

'We're leaving. Tomorrow. Everything has to be packed.'

Richard turns towards her, perhaps about to scream at her, or throw his mug against the wall, but still he seems unable to meet her gaze.

'Are we dead yet?'

'No.'

'You will tell me when we're dead?'

'If I can, Roo, I will.'

She can feel Beauty's bemusement as she approaches and scoops some oats into each of their bowls. Patricia takes her bowl and adds brown sugar – from a fluted sugar bowl that once belonged to her grandmother – and cream, leaving Richard to fend for himself. Sugar will be the death of her, but you have to die of something, and it's better to die of something you like – like pies.

'I was dreaming.'

'Yes?'

'That we were dead.'

7

Patricia starts to eat her oats.

'We were in heaven or hell, I can't say which. I doubt it mattered. All that mattered was that we were dead and we didn't bloody well know it. No one had told us.'

'Who would have?'

'God, probably.'

'Well he won't have, because we're not.'

'We're not?'

'Not quite.'

She has many strategies to silence him. One of them, and often the most effective, is wit.

Richard gives himself sugar and cream, like one who deserves a treat. He has always eaten exactly the same as her, yet he has remained wiry and tough throughout, like a jockey. There is no justice in this – nor in anything else.

'Because it's coming.'

'What is coming?'

'The ambulance. I said I have two dead children for you to pick up.'

'What do you mean two?'

'You know what?'

'No, I don't.'

'You think I'm not here, but I am.'

'Roo, I know very well you're here.'

Patricia has owned the same car for twenty-five years. A cream-coloured Mercedes. Rupert and George ripped the beige plastic panelling off the doors several years ago, leaving the metal of the doorframes exposed, but she has long ceased to notice this. There are more recent tartan rugs and horse blankets covering the back seats, each of which has been shredded. The damage usually takes place when Patricia and Bheki go into the Spar and leave the dogs – paradoxically – to protect the car. They try to attack whoever passes, and then turn on the car as the only alternative.

They have been a familiar sight in the village: the large muddy Mercedes, the agitated dogs, the shy Zulu man in the impeccable dark blue overalls, and the woman emerging, pale and strangely buoyant, her metal walker measuring their progress towards the shop. But in recent years they have started to appear out of place. What was once a working farmers' village — the air full of muck from the former cattle market and the honking of trains carrying timber — has become more upmarket. Surrounding farms are being turned into golfing estates and syndicated trout farms. Small shops selling handmade pottery, woven rugs and leather goods have sprung up. This air of gentility is only disrupted at weekends at the liquor store, when farm workers gather to play mrabaraba and get drunk on quarts of beer.

Bheki is waiting for her at the front stoep after breakfast. He folds the walker and puts it into the boot. Bheki will be driving them down to Durban the next day and has agreed to stay on as their gardener and chauffeur. Patricia tried to send him to a better school when he was still a boy, but it soon became clear that Bheki had no interest in books. What he seemed to love more than anything else was the car, which he would clean for a few rand whenever he had the opportunity. Patricia would let him sit inside the car for whole afternoons, until one day she showed him how to start it up, put it into gear and edge forward. By the time it was becoming too painful for Patricia to drive herself, Bheki had long since attained his licence.

'We have to go across to Mr Ford.'

'Yebo, Madam.'

'While I'm there, perhaps you could take the car to the garage and fill her up. Remember to check the tyres. We have a long journey ahead of us tomorrow.'

'Yebo, Madam.'

Bheki has driven to Durban before. Unlike Beauty, he has seen the sea — but he has never spent more than a few nights outside the boundaries of the farm, let alone lived in a large city. Whenever she has asked him about the move, he has remained evasive, so she has no idea whether it is quiet excitement or dread he feels, or a combination of the two. Bheki rarely speaks to her outside of what is practical.

The driveway of Dwaleni passes the long line of rubble that was once the stables before entering what remains of the paddocks. The road then declines gradually towards the marshlands, passes one of the larger dams and ends in a gum and wattle plantation, where it finally joins the tarmac road. Previously, mountain streams crossed the road in several places, and whenever there was a thunderstorm, sections of the meandering orange driveway would be washed into the bush. But now the road is worse than before: huge corrugated tyre tracks criss-cross it, leading off into the fields to one of the new half-constructed houses. All around are trenches filled with yellow sludge, blasted trees and torn fences. This verdant stretch, which was once a favourite place of Patricia's – a breathing place between the real world and the farm – has been reduced to a war zone, in which men wander about in the mist like wounded soldiers, their boots heavy with mud.

The car labours past lopsided orange trucks, a row of tin shacks that some workers have crudely assembled, and a fire in an old oil barrel. By now the rain has thickened to a steady mizzle and everything is blurred with it. They are just passing out of this nightmare zone and are nearing the marsh when the car slithers off to one side and smacks against a wall of clay and rock.

'Christ, be careful!'

The engine has cut out and for a while they watch the fine rain against the windscreen, the wipers vainly swiping it aside, an exercise in futility.

'You'll have to reverse. Slowly. Otherwise we'll get stuck.'

Without a word, Bheki backs the car and regains the track. It is almost impossible to see out of the steamed-up windows and when a rock clumps dubiously against the bottom of the car, neither of them comments. After that, Bheki drives with exaggerated deliberation and care. If blame is to be attributed – he seems to be implying – it lies with the chaos of the road, or the folly of the builders, or the folly of having builders in the first place.

At the marsh they find a long-tailed widowbird labouring under his heavy wet tail. Red bishops swing in the reeds, their feathers ruffled and fluffed out. A solitary stray donkey stares at them as they pass, his body streaked with wet, making him resemble a quagga. Between Patricia and Bheki, the silence feels deeper than usual. Maybe Bheki will be delighted to see the back of this place tomorrow after all.

Which in clearer moments is her attitude too. The farm, which she inherited from her father when she and Richard made their mismatch, has never managed to make much profit. It's too rocky and – at least in the summer months – too wet. It started to do slightly better only in the seventies, when Patricia decided to breed Welsh ponies and started to take over the management of the farm from Richard. As for Richard, he gave up any pretence at being any good at anything after her father died. Before Richard's illness, he contented himself with little more than a barn full of chickens, a modest dairy herd and some general meandering about.

'Do you think the old man would be unhappy we're leaving?'

Bheki stares ahead, saying nothing to this. It isn't rudeness. Or if it is, it has been so characteristic over the last years that it no longer seems to matter. Bheki tends to let conversation pass him by, like a pleasant breeze occupying an altogether different landscape, and she has developed the habit of using this vacant space to talk freely, as one might with a priest, or – heaven forbid – some kind of analyst.

'Do you remember my father, Bheki?'

'Yebo, Madam. I was already cleaning your car when he passed.'

'I've been thinking a lot about him lately. He might have died too young, but even then he had a full life to look back on. And a great deal to be proud of. He was fortunate in that way. Most of us don't have that, do we?'

Bheki inclines his head but declines to comment.

'He'd also earned it, mind you. Through hard work. And what my mother used to call character. He never complained. He used to say if you don't like it, change it. Don't sit with a problem, feeling sorry for yourself. He was always up at five every morning and he only sat down again at five that evening, usually with a glass of whisky in his hand. And that was when he made himself available to his family and his friends. Oh – and the dinners we used to have at that house! You'll see it, Bheki. The house has a lovely view of the harbour. My favourite view in all the world.'

'I do not like to look at the sea,' Bheki says, barely audible.

'My father only spoke against Richard once – when I said I wanted to marry him. But he gave his consent when he found out I was pregnant, and he never spoke against Richard again after that. Even after he'd seen the disaster he was already making of – everything.'

'They say he was a good man.'

'The one good man in my life.'

Beauty

Even now she is frightened of uBaas. Her fear has always been there. It exists as the mountains around the farm do. It will never be moved and is no longer worth a thought. For the past years, she has had to wash and dress him. She has come to know his body better than anyone – even uMesis. She knows the yellow glowing feet, the tiny black veins running like broken rivers all the way up his legs. Often, in the mornings, he will be aroused as a husband should be for his wife. He never seems to know what to do with himself – and she chooses to ignore it, just as she has chosen to ignore every other shameful thing about him.

These days there is little left of the man he was. He will sometimes call her Mother or Mum. Sometimes she will find him standing in the corridor or sitting on his bed sobbing. Now that all the animals are gone, he seems to be missing them constantly. He will look in every room of the house for the dogs, and sometimes he will go out in search of the cows or ponies or chickens. But still she fears uBaas. Even today — when he can hardly even dress himself — they both know that he is the one with the power over her, and that he will never let either of them forget it.

When the sound of the car is gone, she sits at the kitchen table to have her tea. She likes to use the teacup with the traces of gold around the rim. There was once a picture of the Queen of England on it, but that has been worn away over time and all that remains is a ghost. Drinking from the cup makes her feel simple, clear, strong. She can begin to breathe again, take in the room and decide on what she must do next.

UBaas is in one of the spare rooms, looking through the boxes like he will die if he stops doing it. She doubts he knows what he is looking for. She certainly doesn't. But such a thing doesn't concern her: even before he went mad it was like he was mad. He would mutter to himself as he strode around the farm, forever looking for something to get upset about. He never looked for the reason to be happy, only the thing that could confirm the bad news. Maybe this was because there was only bad news to find, but she has never managed to believe this. There is always a bit of good in everything, even uBaas.

He is sitting on the floor with a box of rosettes on his lap. All around him he has arranged them into piles according to the colours: red, blue and yellow to one side, and orange and green to the other. She is about to turn away and leave him there when she realises he is no longer wearing his trousers. There is nothing unusual about this. He is often getting himself dressed and undressed. He is often preparing himself to leave for somewhere else.

'It's impossible to find anything in this place.'

'Ufunani, Baas?'

'Everything's such a bloody mess.'

Whenever she's alone with uBaas she speaks in isiZulu. It isn't to confuse him. He understands her exactly — even if he doesn't understand much else.

Speaking isiZulu is so much easier for her: it's something she can slip into, like a song.

'Izimpahla zakho?'

UBaas looks at her blankly, perhaps wanting to suggest his clothes have nothing to do with him.

'Mangikusize ukubheka impahla yakho.'

She takes his hand and leads him through to his bedroom. There's no sign of his old corduroys so she takes out tomorrow's pair, which are smarter on account of the journey, and holds them open so he can step in. The trousers are baggy enough to allow his slippered feet to pass through.

'Pull up your zip,' she says in English.

It has always been a joke amongst the workers: uBaas is the one who can never keep his zip up. When he says nothing and doesn't move, she leans forward and pulls it up herself.

Patricia

They have been lovers for over thirty years. It doesn't matter that they have hardly touched in fifteen of them, and that they only see each other every other month: as soon as they're together again, some of their old feeling re-enters the air – a feeling they have never spoken about to anyone, since John was a young English teacher at the school and Patricia a spirited farmer's wife who bred Welsh ponies for other people's children.

These days John Ford looks like an aged dog. Lopsided, softened by whisky and golf. He was once famous for his Hollywood looks, his spin bowling and his temper. The ever-present silver pipe earned him the nick-name Dagga at the school. He has since retired to a house on a windy hill just outside the school grounds, where he lives alone with his television and his books. His wife, who was milder and gentler than he, died of bone cancer several years after he became the headmaster.

Patricia likes to think that she fell in love with him because he was everything Richard was not. John claimed to have read the complete works of Tolstoy twice, while Richard would occasionally page through the *Farmer's Weekly* on the loo. John could recite whole passages from plays Patricia had never even heard of, while Richard could recall only his permanent sense of grievance.

Patricia called herself a Christian for much of her adult life not because she believed in God but because she wanted to be near John, who would stand in the village chapel in his academic gown, his baritone sounding clear above the sweet and disinterested singing of the boys. She liked it when John helped out with Communion. He would dissolve the dry wafer on her outstretched tongue with that cheap sticky wine, the goblet always held just beyond her reach.

As the car comes to a stop on the gravel driveway, he is there to meet her at the front door. He is dressed for golf, which is his way of saying they don't have long. But this suits her: she has no need to linger there. What would be the point? They already said goodbye the previous week, and if it weren't for his phone call last night, in which he said he'd like to see her one last time, she wouldn't be here at all.

Bheki parks as close as he can to the entrance of the yellow-brick bungalow, extracts the walker from the boot and helps lift Patricia from her seat. She is laughing, as usual, to ward off any threat of awkwardness.

'Hello, John. I see you're already dressed for your morning round. How've you been? The mist hasn't cleared.'

'Hello, Trish. Glad you could make it.'

She follows him through the house, which smells of tobacco smoke and shoe polish, and out to the shallow stone-paved stoep at the back. This has been the site of most of their exchanges since John's retirement. In fact, she hasn't been into the bedroom since they last had sex. She can hardly recall when the sex stopped, or how, but there could be no doubt that the decision would have been his.

The veranda stands at the crest of a hill that descends without contradiction all the way down to the village chapel. If the wind is blowing in the right direction on a Sunday morning, you can hear the organ and the drone of familiar hymns. Patricia has long since stopped going to church, but John still attends without fail: the old headmaster, handing out the body and blood of Christ to rows of disbelievers. Patricia liked to joke that she was yet to meet an Anglican who actually believed in God.

Two rows of lime-green pin oaks stand along both borders of the lawn. His wife's roses, which grow along the edge of the stoep, were transplanted from her rose garden at the school. Her rose garden was legendary while it existed, but what was left of it has since been swallowed up by a bank of rhododendrons.

Patricia notices that the roses are in need of dead-heading, but it is their custom never to mention his wife – Anna – even indirectly. The subject tends to leave an aftertaste of disappointment. What light lingers between the two of them has been no match for the afterglow that has grown up around Anna since her death.

'So you're off tomorrow,' he says, already knowing the answer.

'Straight after breakfast.'

'Without a backward glance, I hope.'

'In my experience, backward glances only crick the neck.'

He pours her tea the way she likes it and passes her a Romany Cream. They contemplate the grey dripping void ahead of them. A buzzard appears, flying brokenly, harassed along by two pied crows.

'I was surprised you phoned,' she says. 'Is everything all right?'

'Oh, quite all right. I suppose I was feeling sentimental.'

'You? Sentimental? That doesn't sound like you.'

'Doesn't it?'

He looks at the Romany Creams and decides to take one. This is also unusual: he is generally strict about his diet and takes a grim satisfaction in watching her eat.

'I'll phone you every Sunday evening,' she says.

'You will?'

'To tell you how I'm – surviving Durban.'

As she says this, she imagines he will be relieved to see her go: he will finally be left alone with his wife. There has been a melancholy tone in much he has said and done with her in recent months, and she often feels she has become little more to him than an object of pity.

John has always been a difficult man. At the decisive moment, he has tended to withhold himself. Not only from Patricia, but from Anna, his children, his colleagues, even the boys at the school. It's little wonder he has so few friends and that his two children bolted to Australia. A vain man — she reflects sadly — with little more to offer these days than a few cups of tea and a disinclined ear.

'You don't have to call every week,' he says. 'Only when you have something interesting to say.'

'Well if we wait for that, you'll never hear from me again!'

They laugh, sort of, and sip their tea.

'You've been a good friend,' he tells her.

'As have you.'

He waves her away with a puffed-up brown hand. More like a paw, weathered and leathery and tobacco-stained. Even now his pipe is sitting in his pocket, waiting to be extracted, which he will no doubt do as soon as she has left.

They first met when Patricia brought an unusually clever boy from the farm for an interview. She could see that John was far more interested in her than the silent boy at her side. She was still a radiant laughing woman back then, able to distribute warmth wherever she wished.

'What do you want the boy educated for?' he had asked her, as though the boy wasn't in the room.

'Because he's clever, and I want him to use his cleverness for the general good.'

So John — the facilitator, the fixer — arranged a scholarship for the boy, whose name was Looksmart. But the meetings between the two continued. First in his office, to discuss Looksmart's astonishing progress, and then, for several years afterwards, at the nearby Rawdons Hotel. The rooms were comfortable, the room service affordable and the manager famously discreet.

'Can't you get rid of him?'

'Who?'

'Richard. When you get to Durban.'

'Well what do you suggest I do with him?'

'Send him to a home.'

John has always enjoyed belittling Richard, and he has continued to do so even since Richard's presence has grown so small. John has almost certainly come to think less of her for continuing to harbour her husband. And it still irks her: the way Richard is forever available for mockery while Anna must remain like a saint in stained glass. But then she has been just as complicit in all of this as he.

'I can't do that. Although I suppose I could get a nurse to take care of him. That way I won't have to visit him. All I'd need to do is look across the breakfast table now and again.'

They laugh once more — almost — feeling bad about themselves in a way that is familiar.

'Incidentally,' he says, shifting in his seat like one about to impart bad news, 'I have something I'd like to give you.'

'Oh yes?'

Following his gaze, she sees an envelope on the table, placed there with prominence, even though she has only now noticed it.

'What is that?'

It looks like a letter of resignation, or condolence.

'A letter for me?'

'I'd like you to open it when you get down there. To Durban. But you must promise me not to look at it before that.'

He is looking rather sweet and bashful suddenly: he has never been very good at expressing tenderness. Even their first kiss resembled a mistake: it was something he did as they were getting up, as one of their conversations about the boy Looksmart was officially ended. For a man who has been in control for so much of his life, John's more intimate manoeuvres have always had a lurching, heady quality.

'I'll read it as soon as I've unpacked.'

'Oh don't do that,' he laughs. 'You forget I've seen the inside of your house.'

It takes a long time to die, she thinks, thinking as much about Anna as herself as she angles her body back into the passenger seat. While Bheki folds the walker and nudges it in with the shopping, she stares ahead, feeling annoyed – even though she can't quite place the source of it. In her hand is John's unopened letter, which she stuffs into the cubbyhole, along with all the unopened bank statements from the village postbox. She notices with some satisfaction that John – who has always tried to avoid saying goodbye or even hello – has already slipped back into the safety of the house.

She doesn't know why he summoned her here. To give her that letter? To apologise for himself? To try to explain why he never loved her as much as he loved his wife? Well she didn't think she would ever read his letter. She was tired of him and his unspoken rules and his complacency. Let him go and play golf – and knock that silly little white ball up and down those stretches of grass that never culminated in anything.

The car reeks of petrol, as it does whenever they fill her up, but she and Bheki say nothing about this, nor anything else, on the journey back to the farm. The whole of the Midlands is engulfed in cloud, and the windows of the car are still smeared opaque by the dead dogs' noses.

Beauty

There is too much to do before they go away. In almost every room the floor is filled with boxes, boxes spilling objects from the past whose meaning remains unclear to Beauty. At first the plan was to keep only those things that were of value and in good condition, only those things that could justify their presence in the new house. At least, those had been the words of uMesis. But who was to say what was of value and what was not? Many of the things that were in the worst condition were very old and of the greatest value, and some of the things that were in the best condition, like most of the clothes in the cupboards, were in good condition only because they had never been used.

The removal company would be coming later in the week when the Wileys were gone. Those people would bring down such things as the wheelchair and the last of the boxes. It seemed there would be much more to bring than anyone had imagined. The problem of what to do with the past would have to carry on in the future.

In the last weeks Beauty has been resorting to making the decisions herself: she has thrown away scarves and ties, sheepskin jackets, torn raincoats, dresses for a much thinner Mesis, suits for a more dapper Baas. All of this she has stuffed into bin bags and hauled across to the workers when uMesis is out, or taking a nap, or safely installed at the other end of the house. She knows that uMesis will be grateful for this later. Whenever she has asked uMesis about a this or a that, she is always told to put it aside, they would decide later.

When she is finished with the clearing up after lunch — scraping the remaining chicken bones and roasted vegetables in a chipped enamel dog bowl and stacking the plates at the sink — she leaves the house by the back door. The flyscreen creaks against her, trying to push her back into the house, and then snaps back at her as she slips out, as if now wanting to keep her away for good. Usually at this time Beauty would be eating her lunch under the fir tree, using the mangled wire cage for transporting chickens as her seat, but today it's raining — and anyway she isn't hungry.

UMesis has told Beauty and Bheki that they can have one small suitcase each for the journey tomorrow. The rest of their belongings must be brought up to the house and put into boxes. But when Beauty did her own packing, she found there wasn't much that she wanted to take. The small red plastic suitcase fitted most of her clothes, and one decent-sized box was enough for her towels, bedding and kitchen utensils, as well as all the other things that had been handed down — like the tape deck radio that uMesis gave her when the tape deck got jammed and only the radio part would work.

One of Beauty's favourite possessions is a framed watercolour painting that uMesis gave her, probably because of the cracked glass. It shows an English country lane winding towards a village church. There are sheep filling the road and a dog herding them onwards, its tail a question mark. The picture has been in the family of uMesis for a long time and Beauty likes to keep it above the foot of her bed, so it is the last thing she looks at before she goes to sleep. She doesn't know what it is about the picture that pleases her, but she likes it anyway: the way that remote, long-forgotten scene has been captured in layers of coloured water across the crisp white page.

She walks fast, with her head down, on account of the rain. In her overall pocket is the little cup with the ghost of the Queen on it. All she has ever taken from the house is toilet paper, tea, sugar and sometimes a bit of soap – and this is only when she hasn't been able to get to the shops. The cup is the first thing she has deliberately stolen from uMesis. Of course, she can say to herself that the cup has long ago been forgotten about: uMesis hasn't even seen it for several years because she only ever uses it when uMesis is out. But she knows she is taking a thing that doesn't belong to her and the thought of it makes her feel slightly sick. Yet she can't help herself. It is not only that she likes the cup, with its dainty handle and neat waist, its memory of gold along the rim, the translucency of its china when it is held against the light – she also feels for it. UMesis used to treasure that cup above any other cup, and there was a time she would drink from nothing else.

Beauty has lived all of her life in one of the whitewashed rondavels near the bottom dam. The compound and the blue gums surrounding it have now been levelled, and she and Bheki and a few hangers-on have since moved into one of the half-finished houses at the other side of what was once the dairy. There is no electricity or plumbing yet in the new house and there are no doors or windows, but Bheki put temporary windows and a door into Beauty's room as soon as she moved in.

It has been her dream to have a house of her own. Fifteen years ago, uMesis started up a savings account for the house, and every month uMesis has added a bit more. All Beauty wants is a roof over her head that she can call her own. There will be an extra bedroom for guests and a sitting room where people can come for tea. She will grow her own mealies and other vegetables in the yard and keep some chickens and a goat. She wants the house to be on the road to Giant's Castle and has even gone with Bheki to meet with the Chief to request a plot. Here she will have the same view of the Drakensberg she knows from the farm, but it will be closer – so close that she will be able to see the water streaming down the rock.

The one thing she will not have in her house is a man. There is only one man she could ever have married and that is Bheki. But he has never looked at her in that way before. She has kept her love for him a secret from everyone. The only one to enquire about it has been uMesis, and Beauty immediately denied it. Beauty knows the other workers sometimes called her 'Inyumba' — the barren one — behind her back, but she has learned to live with that.

'Usuphelele umthwalo wakho?'

Bheki is standing in the doorway, his body darker than the darkness of the house. His heavy boots are scuffing the cement, trying to smooth it out. He smells of tobacco and horse. There is a heavy slow presence about him that Beauty, who is half of him in every way — including age — has always drawn comfort from. Bheki is looking at her open suitcase as he might look at a brick — without interest. He doesn't seem to register the source of her guilt: the teacup on the windowsill, glowing like a lamp with borrowed light.

She and Bheki have washed from the same tap and eaten from the same pot since she was a child. Whenever something significant has happened on the farm, they have received the same version of events. Every birth and death has been absorbed at the same moment, under much the same circumstances. She has spent many of her waking hours watching him, thinking about him, looking out for him. And yet there are still parts of the older man that remain a mystery to her. She has no idea, for example, what he really thinks about leaving the farm. Whenever she has tried to ask him, he has shifted away from the subject. All he seems to care about these days is his sick child. A boy of four called Bongani who was born without hearing, pale blue eyes and a white wisp of hair coming from his head. Sometimes it looks to Beauty like there is an old man inside that child, straining to get out.

She asks Bheki where he has been.

'Ngesikhathi uMesis evakashele ishende lakhe mina bengicwalisa uphethiloli emotweni.'

'Wenze kahle,' she says.

'Ubebukeka ekhululekile ngesikhathi emvalelisa.'

She can understand that: why uMesis will be relieved to say goodbye to

John Ford. He is from a time that is long past, and uMesis always comes away from him with that empty lost look on her face, like one over-burdened with bad news.

Patricia

'What are you planning to do with that spade?'

'I'm going for a walk.'

'Then Bheki must come.'

'What for? I'm not a bloody child.'

Richard has been angling to dig her up even before the earthmovers arrived. Her grave is marked by a simple stone, with only her name – Rachel – and a single date marked on it: the date of her birth and her death.

They buried her at the other end of the stables, at the edge of the blood-wood grove behind the hay barn. Often Patricia still asks Bheki to take her there. He drives as carefully as he can over the field, every clump of the grass jolting her ragged nerves. Then he takes out the walker and she picks her way over to the quiet shade of the trees. She stands there in the cool iron-grey light, everything hushed as in a cathedral, the fine dry fronds hissing even with the slightest suggestion of wind. Her heart swells with the sound of those trees, but there is never any sign of Rachel. Just the stone and the breeze, and the great vacant space stretching across the valley, as far as the immovable smoky wall of the Drakensberg.

She might have built the farmhouse on that exact spot had the house not already existed. It was the highest point of the farm, which consisted of a long valley with a swelling of hill at the heart of it – the hill on which the house, the bloodwoods and the farm buildings stood clustered, like wet animals that have crawled onto an island to escape a flood. Each structure was angled in such a way as to suggest they might slip off, back into the dismal current, never to be seen or heard of again.

Instead they have been confined to the first house. One of the first European houses to be built in the area, it was made of local stone, had a long veranda along the front and the usual corrugated iron roof. It was covered in lichen, surrounded by a bottle-green moss and its roots went deep into the earth. Since Patricia had first known the house, it had never had so much as a crack in it, but inside it had always been as dark and dank as any cave.

'There's nothing out there. Just a dirt road with nothing at the end of it. Who would live to hell and gone like this?'

'Us.'

Richard stares hard at her, trying to locate the source of his wife's apparent mirth.

'We're going to the sea tomorrow. We went there once. On your motorbike. While you were still the manager. Do you remember that?'

He took her all the way down to Sheffield beach and buried her in the sand, up to her neck, and he kissed her. There was sand in her mouth, in both of their mouths, from laughing. They stayed up all night, and he lit a fire on the beach and they talked about their lives. His in the north of Yorkshire, growing up with his father – who was a farm manager, like him – because his mother had died of a brain tumour when he was three. Hers in Durban, with her bedroom view of the harbour, and her father at the centre of her life. Her mother also died young, in a car accident while drunk. And so the two of them found a commonality in this, because there was no other. Shortly before the sun came up, they made love: by then there were no more words to say to one another, and making love was about all that was left.

She often thinks of the swim they had afterwards. The sun filtering through the cloud above the sea, the water warm and made of pearly grey light. Just the sea and their naked bodies, their kisses slippery with salt water, and the pale green haze of the hills beyond the shore: the fields of sugarcane in the mist. There hadn't been a soul to disturb their peace.

It was paradise, Richard was paradise, and they have never spoken in quite the same way since.

'That was another man,' he says. 'Not me.'

'Too bloody right.'

Beauty makes her usual appearance and sets the overloaded buckling tea tray down. Before they sold off the remaining ponies, this was the time of day when Patricia would have had them brought in from the fields, and they would have been paraded up and down the lawn so she could examine them. Often they would be released so they could trot about, buck and fart. She would issue instructions, occasionally asking that a horse be brought over. She would step down, using the animal to support herself, her hand running along the silky neck, her fingers touching the velvety snorting muzzle. Sometimes, she would inspect a tooth, or finger a pastern or a hock.

But now there were no more animals. Only one dairy cow for milk — which would be going to Bheki's wife's people at Msinga Top — and some of Richard's chickens — those that had escaped and managed since to survive the civets and the compound dogs. There was also the stray donkey that one of the workers had taken in, but when he left the farm he also left it. Now it roamed freely, feeding off the lush grass and lingering around the rubble where the workers' compound had once stood, perhaps still hoping for its owner's return.

At the arrival of the tea, Richard sits on a plum-coloured step and proceeds to put on his boots. He has owned the same pair for a decade now.

Patricia and Beauty have often laughed about them, saying that it's only a matter of time before they sprouted feelers and walked off.

Every morning before he wakes up, Beauty polishes Richard's boots at the kitchen table and places them outside his bedroom door. Whenever the sole becomes worn through or the stitching goes rotten and rips, she gets Bheki or one of the grooms to patch it up. Patricia doubts there is much of the original boot left. The laces alone must have been replaced half a dozen times. But Richard loves them, and there are few objects these days he remembers. His feet still slide into them without effort: a perfect fit.

Even today Richard's way of telling her he's going out is simply to put on his boots.

'Where are you going?'

Apparently he decides not to answer. His fingers have become tangled in the laces while trying to make what her father used to call a butterfly knot.

'Beauty, I would like Bheki to be with Richard.'

'Yebo, Mesis.'

'Do you know where he is?'

'Yebo, Mesis. I have seen him. I will get him now.'

Beauty circumvents the sleeping Rottweiler and disappears back into the house. Hadedahs caw from a lightning-blasted tree. Richard curses and starts the knot again, not receiving any help from her and certainly not expecting it.

A fresh wave of mist has come in from the mountains and is threading through the trees. In spite of the wetness, Patricia is hoping for a decent-sized storm on her last night. It's unlikely, given the dullness of everything, but she loves nothing more than that rumble of thunder, which always seems to threaten the very foundations of the house.

The lightning in these parts is much feared. It has killed several horses and cattle on the farm – and, when Patricia was a girl, one of the workers. Two years ago, it also killed two schoolboys from John Ford's old school, which made the national news and filled the local papers for a week. The boys had been out on a rugby field, playing golf in the sunlight, when the lightning arrived, literally out of the blue. The cloud came only a moment afterwards, shutting out the sun and bringing a torrent of rain. The two dead bodies lay quite still, their hands almost touching, as the other boys ran for shelter.

Lightning had once struck the farmhouse. A direct hit. Patricia was sitting in the lounge with her Chihuahuas, watching television, when there was an almighty crack that seemed to split the house in two. A ball of blue flame danced across the room and for several hours afterwards there were popping sounds coming from inside the roof. The line of wires threading through the rooms were marked by a thick line of charcoal, and the electrician who came later said the blast should have burned down the house. Since then, the wiring in their house has never been quite the same. Light bulbs frequently explode and sometimes the electricity will surge and cut out.

Rain is not a thing they need very often at Dwaleni. The place is a bog in many places for much of the year, and there are five dams that are fed by reliable springs. They once tried planting wheat but the meagre crop was ruined by fungus. The hooves of the ponies were often infected with canker or thrush. The farmhouse itself has always had an air of damp, with the sheets permanently musty and the wooden floorboards wet. The lining of the curtains was stained long ago by a peppering of black mould that has never since come out in the wash.

She has never been one for tidying up. In most rooms there are cobwebs in the corners of the ceilings, and visitors – in the days they still had visitors – complained of fleas and airlessness, as several of the windows had been warped shut. Except for the occasional lick of paint, which is presently falling back into the garden in uneven, plate-sized chunks, she has kept the house exactly as her father left it. She has said before that if the house gave Richard bronchitis now and again, that was his problem. He had always been welcome to renovate the place himself.

'I think you should take off your boots and go inside for a bath.'

They are lucky if they can get him into the bath once a week – but if he stinks, Patricia doesn't know about it. It has been her technique, perfected over the years, to survive her husband by noticing him as rarely as possible.

'Outside there's a bloody fog.'

'Mist. Will you never learn?'

Richard stands again, threatening for a moment to lunge back indoors – but then he picks up the spade, turns and limps across the garden towards the stables, his boots still under his arm. He has that furtive, loping glee of a baboon stealing mealies. Had there been a gun at hand, she might have taken a shot at him.

'Richard!'

'Beauty!'

'Beau-ty!'

But Beauty has also vanished.

Looksmart

It is still the same sign: Dwaleni Farm. The white drawn-out letters on the blistered tin, tied at an odd angle against the barbed wire fence, as though the name of the farm is still provisional, or the sign has been tacked on as an afterthought.

The letters are a bit faded perhaps, but everything else looks exactly as he left it. The impenetrable shadow of the wattle and gum plantation in the mist, the rattle of the cattle grid as he passes over it, the air of stillness, everything suspended and impossible to comprehend.

He lowers his window and inhales the smell of wet earth and rot. He isn't feeling anything yet: it is still a dream, a world without colour or sharp edges, where everything fades into everything else — and were you to blow at it, it might disappear. If anything, the mist only gets thicker when he switches on his lights and continues into it.

He has been driving for six hours and stopped only for an egg and bacon burger and some strong sweet tea in Harrismith. What seemed like an insurmountable journey has taken up a single afternoon, and a fairly pleasant one at that. He listened to familiar songs from the eighties on the radio, spoke to Noma about tomorrow's Geography test and argued with his wife about – he can't exactly remember what.

The land he lives in is always more various and surprising than expected – and the people friendlier. Yet the sheer scale of the country also unnerved him: hill fading into hill, and the enormous dome of sky, with its thin wash of cloud, textured like elephant hide. The vast stretches of land were marked only intermittently by lines of dark green eucalyptus or wattle, mud-brown cattle filing towards a dam to drink, and top-heavy powerlines marching towards a precarious future. At the new Shell Ultra City in Harrismith, he ate his lunch at a large tinted window that looked down on a gathering of farm animals in a pen: chickens, ducks, a mauled-looking peacock and some ravenous wild-eyed goats. No doubt put there for the distraction of passing children, they were dwarfed by the perpetual passing of the traffic – and looked very far from home.

He has a shameful secret: even today, he's unaccustomed to the freedom he's been given to drive around the country and go wherever he likes. Whenever he sits down in a restaurant or cinema, surrounded by white people, a part of him still expects someone to ask him politely to leave. It is a thing he could never mention to his daughters or even his wife. They would laugh at him and accuse him of making it up. Yet it is a thing he feels: he is an intruder in his own land, condemned to arriving at places where he will never quite belong.

Sighing with something like grief, he lets the car roll forward, the stones popping under the fat tyres. A donkey emerges in the middle of the road, only one shade darker than the mist, and it refuses to move, even when he hoots. It stares him down, almost inviting him to run it over – so he eases the car forward and, just as he is about to nudge the animal with the bumper, it moves aside, and allows him to pass, his side mirror almost brushing its flank.

As a boy, he experienced the Wileys' driveway as a rolling sea, with half-glimpsed horizons before another treacherous descent. On occasion he would trot ahead of the vehicle that was supposed to be transporting him. In those days he could run barefoot along a farm track like this for hours without getting particularly tired. His body was light, his breathing easy, and there was a spring in his step that he assumed would be there forever. But now the driveway has been rubbed out beyond recognition: there are trenches running away from it, puddles, dumped boulders, zigzagging tyre tracks. In places, the road seems to vanish altogether, or go off in different directions into the mist, as if an elaborate labyrinth is under construction. Of course, none of this surprises him. He is expecting to see evidence of the building: he knows it has been going on for exactly three months. It is the apparent disorder of the place that disturbs him: the project he has been managing for more than a year already appears to have failed and been discarded.

He told himself that he would be coming here out of hate. Or, more accurately, out of nostalgia for a time when he could hate properly. For a period, his hatred was his most reliable companion. It was the one thing that could still be found in him whenever he got up in the morning. It burned in him like rage, but was more patient and subtle, and constantly it would drive him to new heights. At times he thought his success would not have been possible were it not for his stamina for hate. But everything that has come to him since – the twin girls especially – has come in the twilight years that have followed his period of hate. These days he recollects his hatred with fondness and some regret, as a race he was once fit and lean enough to run.

He puts the car in park and switches off the engine, letting down the other three windows simultaneously. Something inside the engine whirrs on for a while – but when it stops the silence he knows so well returns to him in all its fullness and sweetness. He once again experiences a surge of grief, coming like nausea, involuntary and from deep within his gut. He swallows it down, clears his throat, breathes in the treacherous wet air.

It isn't too late. He could still turn around and check into his hotel – Granny Mouse's Country House, of all the names in the world – and he could phone home and recite the usual apologies to his wife. He doesn't exactly know what he's doing here, sitting inside this car, which seems so alien to him suddenly — pointing towards the farmhouse like a large silver bullet, ticking with heat.

Did he come here because of the Wileys or because of Grace? He has spent almost half his life trying to get as far away from Grace as possible, but now that he's here, he wants her back, he wants to see her coming towards him out of the mist. Even in death she is still more powerful than he will ever be. She is like a virus capable of wiping out whole villages. And with the prospect of her comes the luxury of his old hate, which starts to filter back into his blood, thick and fragrant.

He doesn't know — even now — whether he has enough hatred left in him for this encounter. Life in the city has softened him, his daughters have softened him, time has softened him. But the old woman will be gone tomorrow and he knows there is only one night left. There can be no question of letting her slip past him — of sparing her, or of sparing himself.

Patricia

The sound of the car comes to her through the mist. An indistinct moan, far off, like the ancient bull calling out from beyond the marsh. She hears it but she does not register it: she is too lost in the objects around her, like the old Pentax camera, which looks well used but is almost entirely unfamiliar, so long ago it is since she last operated it – or even knew how to do so. Inside, there's a half-finished film and she wishes she knew what images had been captured there, but it's too late now, for she has already obliterated the images by opening the camera up.

Everything around her feels muted. Even the bright crimson evening bag that once belonged to her mother has been drained of its redness. Inside, she finds a used ticket stub for a play called *Dream of the Dog*, which once played in London but has no doubt long since been forgotten about. A rubbish bag is sitting next to her wheelchair, waiting for its load of junk, but there's an overall numbness, a feeling of vacancy, a weight in the arms, that makes it seem impossible to move. She thinks once more of burning down the house.

Were Rupert and George alive, they might have heard the car and slipped out, but Ethunzini sleeps on.

'Beauty!'

Half an hour ago, she heard the flyscreen, followed by a clattering of pots – but Beauty would not be Beauty if she didn't need the usual summoning up.

'Beau-ty!'

She measures the progress of Beauty's feet along the corridor and wonders how they will sound in the new house. In spite of her back, she has decided to live upstairs: in the emerald-green light, with its sunbirds and silver-blue glimpses of sea. A lift has already been installed on the staircase for previous tenants. Recently it was attached to a generator for when the power cut out. As for Richard, he will sleep in what was once the library at the back of the house: it will be cooler for him down there, especially in the summer, and it will mean they'll each have a different view.

'Richard has gone off again. With the spade.'

'What must I do, Mesis?'

'Get him. Or get Bheki to get him.'

'I will go.'

'Ngiyabonga.'

The thought of the bloodwood grove returns to her again. The hillock with its mound of moss, wild strawberries and clover, and the small skull of her child, as fragile in the earth as a buried bird's egg.

'And Beauty? Go to Rachel first. Then you can check where the stables, the dairy and the chicken shed used to be. You know what happens when he can't find the animals. He goes out to look for them. He tries to herd them back in from the hills.'

Beauty almost smiles. 'Yebo, Mesis.'

In the front garden, the Rottweiler has finally started to bark. It is not a sound Richard would have provoked, or anyone else who is known to the farm.

'Mesis?'

'It's probably one of the builders wandering about.'

Patricia lifts herself from the wheelchair and lowers herself very carefully into her armchair. Beauty waits and then moves the wheelchair off to a tactful distance before she goes over to the sash window and peers into the mist.

'What is it?'

'There is a big silver car standing under the tree. Angimboni umshayeli.'

'Well, it can't have driven there itself. Maybe the driver has gone around the back.'

'Must I go and look?'

'It's probably one of the developers. It's Richard I'm more concerned about. Someone needs to find him and bring him in. If not you, then Bheki. All right?'

'Yebo, Mesis.'

Beauty leaves the house through the front door and Patricia pictures her hesitating on the stoep. She likes the way Beauty tends to lean towards a thing before approaching it, allowing her body to feel its pull, and moving forward only when her heart is in it.

Ethunzini's muttering continues as Beauty steps into the garden. Patricia can hear that the old dog is no longer responding to anything out there but is expressing a general discomfort back at himself.

'Beauty!'

'Beau-ty!'

She is about to call out for a third time when the flyscreen at the back of the house creaks open, appears to consider its next move, and snaps back shut.

Two

Richard

He has been wading through the grey air for – how long? – when he finds the line of bloodwoods. He understands this track, has travelled it his whole life, so he hardly needs to think. He knows the dairy is at the other end of those trees. It will be a darker oblong in the mist, smelling of cow muck and warm milk, humming with machinery, murmuring with cows. His form of bliss. Somewhere to disappear into: the lines of cows in their stalls, the milk sloshing along the glass pipes, the women in their blue overalls ushering in the next batch. No one ever talks to him there. Too much noise is in the air and there is too much to do. It's the one place where everything runs smoothly, where you can always measure the same result: one hundred cows each producing ten litres of milk a day, always leaving the milk tank full. Nothing else is like that. Even with a chicken you never know what you'll get: sometimes one or two eggs in a day, sometimes none.

But where the encouraging oblong of dark is supposed to be, he finds only stackings of corrugated tin, wooden beams, bricks and mortar piled up in a long trench. There is a large concrete sink that he recognises as coming from the storeroom, but the taps are gone. Actually, the whole bloody storeroom is missing. Inside the sink he discovers a dark turd. Baboon? Human? It looks like a statement of sorts, so neatly placed. But what is it saying? And to whom?

At the other end of the rubble, he finds a door and a doorframe miraculously preserved. The door is still standing, slightly ajar. He climbs over a mound of broken concrete and rusted metal rods and kicks the door open with his boot. There he sees something like the waiting pen, but where the cows should be standing, knee-deep in bog, he finds only weeds, a whole crop of them, and realises that a long time has passed since this war – or whatever it was – took place. So where has he been hiding in the interim?

And where have all the animals gone? His herd of cows, the barn full of chickens. Is this something the old bitch has achieved? She was always jealous of his activities on the farm. Did she blow up the buildings with all the animals inside? With her, anything is possible: there is no end to her malice. He tries to lift a lump of cement to see what's underneath, but it doesn't even shift. What lies buried beneath it will have to stay there, at least until he can get hold of a tractor or a truck.

He sits down in the doorway, facing the weeds, and tries to piece together what he knows: the air too thick to see in, the farm lying in ruin, all the animals gone. It happened a while back, the destruction, and he has been away since. All of this took place in his absence, or because of his absence, and is probably the workings of the bitch. For a moment he gets the whiff of a glorious idea, but then he sees his boots have been recently polished and he realises no: she can't possibly be dead.

She probably sent him on some errand. She might have intended for him to come upon all of this. The dead under the line of rubble, the doorway leading to no cows, even the turd in the sink. And now that he's here, what's he expected to do? He senses an opportunity to step away from what he was supposed to do, and do what he wants to do – but what does he want to do?

Then he feels the same familiar ache in his blood, the faint ringing in his head, and the sound of her voice, coming like a hard little lamb bleat across the hills.

Rachel.

He says this, not knowing whether he is thinking the word or saying it.

Oh, Rachel.

He remembers the tall grey trees around her, hissing like a broken sea.

Where have they hidden you?

There's no doubt in his mind that she's calling for him from under the earth. There are stones where her eyes should have been, a root inside her mouth. What age is she? He has often wondered this. What does she look like now? Sometimes she comes to him in dreams. A girl of three, upright and radiant as a dancer, gnawing a raisin bun. Sometimes as a grown woman with a head of dark and heavy hair, bearing his child. Sometimes she even comes as his imaginary son – and once as a half-crazed hag dragging him back into a place of darkness. But most often she is the infant she was on the only day he saw her.

Looksmart

The lights at the back of the house are off, and he wonders whether he might have got the dates wrong – and whether or not the old woman has left. Where are the dogs, for instance? The security lights surrounding the house? He would have expected the Wileys to defend themselves better, or at least to give the appearance that they had something worth defending. Yet the farmhouse stands entirely available to him, with not even the back door locked.

But he did hear the Rottweiler out front, which means that someone is living here. And there can be no question that they would have left the dog behind – not that particular one. Yet how could that dog be alive still? In the morning, he will have to work it out. Perhaps he was only hearing things: it may have been the sound of the dog's long-departed ghost haunting the front garden, not even giving up its post after death.

There is an eerie pale blue light in the kitchen and it takes him a while to see that there's a pot bubbling on the stove, smelling like dog food. It's unlikely the Wileys would be eating such a concoction for their supper. He remembers how the couple would eat three-course meals three times a day and throw all their scraps to the dogs.

The kitchen looks smaller than he envisaged, and humbler. The wooden breakfast table with the dark green legs is still there, a circle burned in the middle of it by a pot, and the linoleum floor has been worn down to the cement around the kitchen sink. The charred-looking wood-fuelled AGA is still there too, but standing cold, and the usual yellow fly strips, covered in dead flies, hang from the ceiling – but reminding him now of the Buddhist prayer flags his daughters Noma and Nondumiso have hung across their bedroom ceiling.

There is a distinct smell of gas, but Looksmart does nothing about it. Nor does he try to switch on the lights. He stands in the gloom, wondering whether he is about to be shot.

'Beauty!'

He smiles, feeling self-conscious, like one who knows he is being watched. The old woman is still there, still calling the girl like she's calling one of her dogs.

'Beau-ty!'

If the old man is about, it is more than likely he is about to be shot. But Looksmart can't detect his presence here. The house is too still, too settled into itself. The old man would always stir up everything around him, infect everyone with his air of crisis, his potential for rage, his habitual disappointment. No, this feels to him more like a – not unpleasant – peasant's house. Maybe Beauty and her extended family have moved in and confined the old man to one of the farm huts. He finds himself cheered by the prospect of the old man's death. He has no idea what his age might actually be – he always seemed so ancient – but his death seems likely, since men rarely live as long as women. In the end, they are made of weaker stuff, weaker bones and nerves and blood.

The corridor has an echoing, dripping quality, and the same smell it had when he was a boy: stuffy and dank, like a wet animal, more horse than dog.

Still it feels like a place that has never experienced the sun.

'Beauty, is that you?'

She sounds exactly the same: as if it is beneath her dignity, or not worth her while, to be frightened — and as if she can take whatever comes her way in her stride.

There is light spilling into the corridor from the sitting room. It seems to be the only light left in the house. The rest is in darkness, like parts of the brain that have shut down. The sitting room was always her favourite place, her nest. The light has a strange effect along the walls: it makes the walls look like they are sprouting black hairs. Only after a moment does he register these as picture hooks, and as soon as he does the images that once hung there come flooding back to him: Patricia holding a Welsh pony at the Royal Show with several sashes around its neck, Patricia as a little girl in the Durban house being pushed in one of those hooded prams with the large wheels and sprung suspension, Patricia clinging to a Great Dane, and Patricia slightly older, sitting in a paddle pool in a large hat with a smear of cream along her nose. She was always on the podgy side, but now and again, under the gaze of her father, she could appear almost beautiful.

But most distinctly he can recall a picture of Richard, crouched in front of a pair of leopards he shot in Kenya. The young man is gazing vacantly over the photographer's shoulder, apparently detached from his casual act of violence. The treated skins were later draped over the leather couches in the sitting room, and as a small boy Looksmart wanted them. He would hold the heavy dry paws in his hands and squeeze his fingers through the bullet holes.

His first reaction to her is physical: a lurch through the body, as when one witnesses a shocking event: a car accident on the side of the road, a hideous injury, an arm hanging off, or half a head — a thing that seems impossible to look at but has to be looked at twice.

She is doing nothing more than sitting there in a chair, smiling with habitual politeness, dimly expectant and alert. Where everything in the house seems smaller, she looks larger, swollen outside of the space he might have assigned for her — and older and greyer, with colourless floating hair, and eyes pushed deep back into her face. Her skin is dull and puffy and covered in a fine down, and her feet are bare and propped up on a box, the toes sticking out at odd angles, like the teats of a cow.

'Hello?'

Only her voice has remained unchanged, filled with its usual potential for authority and scepticism. She is always looking for the joke, Patricia, the thing to laugh at, the thing to steer her gaze away from the unbearable present.

'Who is that?'

He remains in the doorway, just out of reach of the light, and studies her. She is sitting in the same chair, facing the same mantelpiece. The standard lamp with its squiff shade is giving out a greenish pool of light, and all around her is chaos. It looks like someone has stood where he is standing and thrown boxes and bits of furniture in every direction but hers. Framed pictures are stacked against the walls, with paler rectangles on the walls marking the places where they once hung, and yellowing documents and photographs spill from the tin trunks and half-packed boxes. There is what looks like a disused wheelchair standing by the door and on the table next to her, just caught inside the ring of light, is a Granny Smith apple and a wooden-handled knife. The leopard skins are no longer there, but there is a Nguni cowhide that is new — stippled exactly like the half-recollected picture of the Great Dane in the hall.

'Good evening, Madam.'

He says this in a voice he barely recognises — and finds he is unable to step forward into the light. He would like to stand there and look at her for a long time, and then leave the house, and drive off without another word. That would be enough: to have seen her and seen what she has become. Was that not revenge enough?

But what is stranger still — and it is a thing he never prepared himself for — is that she doesn't immediately seem to recognise him. Of course, he is standing in the dark, not using his voice — but still he never anticipated this moment of standing before her like a stranger.

He is used to seeing her delight at seeing him. Her world was always put on hold whenever he came into this room. But it has been many years —

almost twenty-five, in fact – since they were last in each other's company. Too many days now separate them. All he is to her at that moment is a darker place in the darkness, dense with possibility.

'What do you want?'

Even if he wanted to, he finds he can't begin to answer this.

They each wait for the other to speak. She is still looking towards him as if he is no one – a plumber or someone come to fix the roof – and there is nothing about him, and his whiff of the outside world, that could ever have anything to do with her.

'The dog. It is still there.'

'Which dog?'

'The Rottweiler. Chloe, you called it. Still there on the stoep. How is that possible?'

'That one is Ethunzini.'

'Ethunzini? Chloe's puppy, perhaps?'

'No. Chloe died before she could have a pup.'

He feels the years stretching inside him, between the young man he was and the man he is now, and he sees the years stretching all around him: Patricia's days in this room alone, that lamp going on and off, the fire being lit and going out, the light appearing at the window and then fading away again – thousands of days lived without him, and he experiences the stirrings of a sensation like guilt.

'It doesn't matter,' he tells her – in something more like his old voice, the voice of his boyhood. 'It's still the same dog.'

'Do I – know you?'

Only now does he step into the room and make himself available to her gaze.

Patricia

She knows from the sound of the flyscreen that something is wrong, that someone has entered the house in a way that is irregular. It is not the sound of a farmer's or a worker's boots, but a kind of clacking, more like a woman's high-heeled shoes – yet it is also a man's tread, deliberate and leisurely. She hears him reach the corridor, sauntering like he's at a museum, viewing artefacts from another era, in spite of the fact that it's dark down there and there can be nothing to see.

There is a readiness in her that has been learned over time that protects her from anything resembling fear. She almost has an appetite for it, this confrontation with a man with no face, who steps into her house uninvited, makes himself at home and decides on ways of taking back from her. She finds a steely quality running through her now, and a resignation to her fate. It isn't that she's afraid of pain – she has grown quite accustomed to that – but she knows she wouldn't want the shame of it.

It isn't something she likes to go on about, but these days she's in almost constant pain: a dull ache all along her spine that at times radiates as far as her fingertips, thinning the air around her, leaving a metallic taste in her mouth that no amount of tea can ever quite eliminate.

It gives her an abstract air, this pain. It makes her feel she has no substance in the world, and is adrift, suspended in space, forever on hold. For much of the time, she is trying to manoeuvre herself away from the pain – but it is always there to meet her, at every turning.

The man is standing at the door, wearing what appears to be a suit.

'Good evening, Madam.'

The word 'Madam' sounds immediately absurd, consciously absurd, intended to suggest, perhaps, that Patricia's reputation has preceded her. But her reputation for what, exactly?

'What do you want?'

He looks deeper into the ramshackle room and says something she can hardly hear about a dog. It sounds like a veiled threat, aggrieved and accusatory, but it is also uncertain – as if speaking for this man is still a kind of experiment.

'Which dog?'

'The Rottweiler. Chloe, you called it. Still there on the stoep. How is that possible?'

'That one is Ethunzini.'

'Ethunzini? Chloe's puppy, perhaps?'

'No. Chloe died before she could have a pup.'

'It doesn't matter. It is still the same dog.'

And it's only at that moment that she recognises his voice – although she can't quite believe it at first.

'Do I – know you?'

'You might have thought so once.'

He steps into the room, his features seeming to dissolve and loom, morphing into a thing they are and are not, and in that instant she knows him.

'But I am Looksmart.'

He uses the word strangely, as a proposal of sorts.

'Is it just possible you remember me?'

'Looksmart!' she says at last, finding her voice, finding her breath to speak. 'Why — you've come back!'

They seem to gasp inwardly, but are both apparently uncertain as to what to say or do next. Too much lies between them. And for reasons that are not yet clear to her, Patricia knows even now that anything they might say to one another will be dangerous, difficult.

'How well you look!'

'Madam,' he says again, 'I am a different man.'

'You certainly seem different. You're wearing a suit.'

She means this as a compliment, but he seems to take immediate offence.

'That is what I am like these days. I wear a suit.'

He stands there, as proud as he used to look in his school uniform. The suit is beautifully cut and the tie neatly knotted — although perhaps too flagrant a red for Patricia's taste. He still looks to her like someone in service, wearing his suit with defiance, but secretly being chafed at the collar.

She can see at once that he is trying to be rude, that he came here having already decided to be rude, yet it also seems that he hasn't yet found his voice for it, or his theme. He was once such a polite boy, enthusiastic and chatty, but then he went underground — disappearing long before he finally went.

'I never thought I'd see you again. Where on earth have you been?'

Instead of answering, he waves away an imaginary fly and comes deeper into the room, his steps tentative, like one walking on ice. She supposes he wants her to see how he is 'these days' — able to walk into any room without invitation.

'I must say,' she says, 'it took me a moment to recognise you, Looksmart. How have you been keeping?'

'Is that because I'm wearing a suit?'

It is not the suit that strikes her as irregular, but his way of wearing it. He seems to be too conscious of it, as if he's wearing it as some form of disguise — or as a calculated affront.

'How long has it been? It must be twenty years. Longer? I have long ago given up trying to do the maths – on anything. I find it only ever leads to the same result.'

She wishes she knew the words to bring him back. The secret phrase that might unlock him and end this apparent pantomime. But he continues to disregard her, wandering across to the mantelpiece, where he runs his finger along it like one carrying out moves he's rehearsed in his head – a way of coming into the room that doesn't quite seem to fit now that he's doing it. He fingers the dust, perhaps imitating a scene from a film, a sergeant major inspecting the barracks with an air of exaggerated disappointment.

'Times have changed,' she says, 'haven't they?'

He looks affronted by this statement – in spite of the fact that she hardly knows what she might mean by it.

'Oh yes,' he says, sarcastic – and still ridiculous. 'Although I see you're still here where I left you. Only a bit smaller than I pictured you. And not half so frightening.'

'Frightening? But I was never that.'

She can't but feel hurt by this, misrepresented – not only by what he's saying but by his complete disregard, a disregard that extends beyond his words and to his whole body. He seems already to have turned against her, long before he even entered this room.

'You know I had to look up to you once,' he carries on. 'I was – what?' He considers and then indicates with his hand, his fingers pressed together and pointing upwards in the African way. 'I was about this high.'

'When you left, you were a great deal taller than that.'

He shrugs, perhaps to tell her that his height was hardly the point, after all – and then he moves off again, across the room, towards the large dark windows that look onto the former dog-run. But there's nothing to see outside of the house: only the light of the room reflected back at them.

'Wouldn't you like to sit?'

'Thank you, Madam,' he says, sounding pensive but still important, 'but I think I'd prefer to stand.'

Only the other day she was thinking about him. She was looking through what she calls 'the original boxes'. They had made their way up from Durban after the death of her father and she had never before had the strength to unpack them. They were stacked in one of the spare rooms, a room it was unlikely anyone had entered for several months – except perhaps for Beauty, who might have ventured in there with a vacuum cleaner or a feather duster, more to show her face than to clean anything up.

The yellow curtains were always closed at the far end of the room, and the single speckled light bulb barely lit what stood beneath it – let alone the far corners, which harboured spiders the size of her hand, for all she knew. In her father's day, this was the best guest bedroom of the house. It had an adjoining bathroom – the large clawfoot bath made of metal took half an hour to run and remained warm for an hour afterwards – and a bay window looking out on the side garden. Admittedly, there was never much of a view: the trunks of a few fir trees, the wire fence, the dirt track that leads around the house, and the odd glimpse of the hill that separates the farm from John Ford's school – but it was once a good room nonetheless, with its own fireplace, a solid four-poster that came from the Durban house, and the antique cupboard containing the coats of great-grandparents that had probably never been worn since their arrival in South Africa.

When she saw the fishing rod sticking out from under the bed, in a red cotton holder, the segments tied together with black ribbon, it made her lurch internally – even though at first she didn't know why. Alongside it, she discovered a sky-blue fishing box, which was filled with reels knotted with line and old lures with glaucous red eyes, rusted barbs and bits of pearly glitter streaming away from them – still as sparkly as they must have looked in the shop.

At first she thought the tackle belonged to one of the boys who had passed through the farm – a brother of a girl who had bought a Welsh pony, perhaps, or one of the boys who used to visit the farm from John Ford's school in order to fish. There had been several such boys over the decades – their names all forgotten now, their young bodies no doubt lapsed into the indignity of middle age, their disappointing wives probably just as disappointed in them. But then the meaning of the red holder – its black ribbons so exemplary, the way they had been tied and double knotted, like shoelaces

on a Sunday morning – came right back to her. She undid the knots that only Looksmart could have made with his child's fingers and extracted the dark red fibreglass rod, with its comic cork handle and its tip bent from where it must have been shut in a cupboard or a door.

It was without question the rod she had bought for Looksmart, the rod he'd used to catch his first fish and that – at least as far as she knew – had never been used again. At that moment, the black ribbons, double knotted, took on a fresh significance.

'You know I was thinking –'

'Oh yes?' he says, all ironic, 'and when was that?'

'Only the other day – I was thinking about the day you caught your first fish.'

'My first what?'

'I wonder if you remember that?'

He turns away from the black glass, looking suddenly haggard, like a man who has forgotten to eat for a week. She wonders if this is a temporary expression, brought about by the strangeness of this visit, or if he's permanently like this: characterised by a general illness that has its origins not in her but in the life he has led since he left her – that series of events too numerous and inscrutable to comprehend.

'Because I can picture it like it was yesterday.'

'Like it was yesterday, hey?'

As he speaks, she recalls the times he used to tease her, when teasing – no doubt learned in part from her – was the mode between them. At the time, their world seemed to permit little else: it didn't even allow them to touch. But now there is no affection in this echo of their old style. Today everything between them seems to bristle with innuendo and hurt.

'You caught your first fish at the bottom dam. I bought you a little red fishing rod and taught you to cast on the front lawn. Don't say you don't remember that!'

'But I really don't remember it.'

In those days her back was already starting to niggle her, but she was able to ride a horse and stride across the field of overgrown kikuyu where the Welsh ponies grazed – jumping over ditches, her lungs filled with laughter. That long field is still there today, running all the way from the driveway down to the bottom dam, but much of the kikuyu has become overgrown with bugweed and indigenous scrub – and more recently the earthmovers have reduced it to a swamp.

But how vividly she recalls that afternoon. She and the boy setting off from the house, across that field. He running ahead of her, the red fishing rod held up like a spear, and she following behind with the fishing box, a blanket and their picnic lunch.

The thunder was already starting up, and she recalls worrying briefly about that raised rod, so like a lightning conductor, such a temptation for the gods. But they made it down without incident, arriving at the small muddy dam as though it were the most magical fishing place in the world. At least – that is how she remembers it.

'We went down there to fish one afternoon.'

'As I say, Madam. My mind is a blank.'

'You were so light on your feet. Like a little bird – made out of twigs.'

'I was made out of twigs?'

'You know what I'm saying.'

'Not really, Madam.'

Looksmart is as sullen as the sky that afternoon, looking down on the scene as though it were only there to taunt him.

'The hook kept getting caught everywhere. The grass, your hair. Even your ear once. But you kept on going, determined to get a bite. And then at last – you did! You were so excited, you turned and ran, you ran all the way up the riverbank with the fish bumping up behind you!'

How they'd laughed. But now that she looks at him, she wonders if she might have imagined it – or at least embellished the event with other events, featuring other boys from the past. Is it possible she has brought all her memories together into this one boy – the one boy who stood out?

He is smiling at her oddly.

'That was your first fish,' she says. 'Please don't say you don't remember it.'

He says nothing: but this time he does not deny it.

'You said how beautiful it looked, lying there in the dead grass. And then, just as the rain was starting up, you decided: we had to return it to the water. So you picked it up and you lowered it back. It wallowed there for a while, its belly facing upwards like it was dead, and we thought it was too late, that it had drawn in too much oxygen, but the gills were still sort of drifting, and eventually it righted itself and struggled forward – and then it flicked its tail and disappeared.'

'If I remember myself correctly,' he says, 'I would have wanted to eat that fish.'

'But you were a gentle child, always wanting to please.'

He lets out a sound like laughter and turns away.

'Don't you mean always wanting to please you?'

Beauty

The car is so covered in mud that it looks like it was born from the earth. It is parked in a way that suggests the driver has been here before: it is parked exactly where uMesis asks her visitors to park, firmly inside the garden and under the tree, but not blocking the gate to the stables and allowing enough space behind it for other cars to enter. She notices that the gate has been left open, however, which suggests either a person from the city or someone who knows all the animals are already gone.

She can feel the heat still coming from the car as she approaches it. It is not a car she has seen before. It looks new under its dirt and not intended for these roads. Through the darkened glass she can hardly see inside, but there is a small red light flashing with urgency near the steering wheel and another light pulsing on the passenger seat with a slower, more deliberate blue. The lights give the car an air of importance, connecting it to places Beauty can barely imagine. As she stands there the blue light leaps into life and a chirpy song starts up. It is the driver's phone, which he either forgot in the car or chose to leave behind. But she draws comfort from the song: it sounds like an advertisement for something harmless, like a mattress or a couch.

Retreating from the car, she leaves the garden through the front gate. The bloodwoods are soon around her, dripping in the darkness, as she meets the deep clay path that circumvents the house. Reed frogs are singing merrily from the marsh, almost on the other side of hearing. At her passing in front of a security lamp, Ethunzini lets out a single disinterested bark.

She steps into the heart of a puddle that would not usually be there, and meets the original road to the dairy. Beauty never curses if there is anyone about, but when alone she occasionally gives vent to her frustration, and will find herself growling deep inside her like the Alsatians once did. She will do this only for a moment, standing quite still, for even her fury is discreet. Afterwards, she will continue like nothing has happened, sweeping up the plate that might have smashed, or remaking the bed of uBaas for the fifth time that day. But now she doesn't growl at the puddle: she is already as wet as a person can be.

Because the trucks have so mauled the track around the house, she has recently started to use a torch to get back to her room at night. But tonight it doesn't matter that she has forgotten it: she likes the darkness and the sound of the rain in the darkness. As she runs through the storm, it feels like a blessing is passing through her.

There is no evidence of uBaas. There is only the sound of the rain and the reed frogs, sounds you soon forget to hear if you don't remind yourself about them. Sometimes, uBaas will cry out for no clear reason, and she is able to discover him. At other times he will be standing quite still, and you can pass him close enough to touch him without seeing him. But whether he is being silent or not, there is always an argument going on inside his head.

It didn't take long to see that the new houses that were being built across the farm were much the same as the first house. Each house had the same long stoep along the front and a similar arrangement of rooms behind it. The spaces for the windows were larger and there were fewer walls, but it seemed that each new house was an effort not to forget the original house — or otherwise each was an attempt to refresh it.

Beauty has been sleeping in what she thinks of as uBaas's room, the room to the left of the entrance that was once the study of uMesis's father. That was back when the farm was still more or less functioning, although it is said that the farm has never made much of a profit. The name Dwaleni means 'built on rock'. It is like the story from the Bible: nothing much ever manages to grow there.

There is no sign of Bheki, but this is not surprising. Since the birth of his child it has been his habit to slip away when off duty: it is understood that sometimes he likes to be alone. Beauty has never been able to speak to Bheki about his child. He loves the boy with a quiet determination that goes past the place where any words can reach. She has often wondered whether he knows anything about what has been said about the child: that it is the result of a curse, of dark magic. The reputed cause is the boy's mother, Phume, whose father is said to be both a nyanga and a priest at Msinga Top. Bheki once described the homestead where the father lives to Beauty: it is high up in the mountains, often surrounded by mist, and the huts are painted the colour of a kingfisher. When Bheki went there, there was a dead crow wired to a post at the entrance to the yard. Phume's father preaches on Sundays in a long whitewashed building along the bottom of the homestead and during the rest of the week he makes muthi in a hut at the back. He uses water to heal and is known to have killed several water tokoloshes, which he lures with muthi and mirrors to the edge of the river where they dwell: on seeing their own reflections, it is said they immediately die.

Beauty regards the activities in a nyanga's hut with the same suspicion with which she regards the exotic names and incantations she has encountered in church. She has also felt uncomfortable around Phume since she made her first appearance as a worker in the dairy. The woman said she felt the presence of ghosts and wouldn't go anywhere without rock salt in her pocket, which she would throw ahead of her to ward away the malevolent spirits. She said all the women who lived on the farm were visited by tokoloshes at night, including uMesis, and that they were condemned to barrenness and dead children as a result.

So when the mysterious boy Bongani was born, people talked. Phume took the child back to her father at Msinga Top, but the cure seemed to have no effect. The child's appearance never changed and his parents came to accept that he would never be able to speak. She has often wondered about the meaning of the child. It is possible he has no meaning: it is possible the ancestors — or whoever decides such things — simply hand out destinies indifferently. Perhaps the only real justice in the world is the one you make for yourself.

Beauty wipes the mud from her feet with newspaper and changes into another pair of overalls and a pink anorak. The anorak she inherited a long time ago from one of the stable girls from England — one of the ones uMesis never liked to talk about. She can hardly picture the girl any more: not her name, her voice, or even the year she came. All she can recall is the girl's cropped hair and pale complexion, her body narrow and small as the body of Grace. These days the pink anorak is the only proof that the girl ever existed.

It appears to be raining even harder than before, so she leaves the house through the front entrance at a steady trot, passing the place on the stoep where Ethunzini would have been sitting. She maintains this pace all the way along the ruins of the dairy and farm buildings, slowing only when she has reached the fir tree that stands outside the kitchen. There she finds two of uBaas's chickens huddled against the steps, but she nudges them back into the night and slips through the flyscreen before they can think to dart into the warmth of the house.

Immediately she hears voices coming from the sitting room. It sounds at first like an argument is taking place, but then she hears a man's laughter. She can tell even from the kitchen that it is not the laughter of uBaas. He has never been able to laugh with any openness: the best he's ever managed is a kind of snuffle, as if humour is dangerous and by laughing he might suffocate.

She has two ways of coming down the corridor: one that uMesis can hear and one she can't. The way that can't be heard requires her to walk along the wall on one side of the corridor and then to switch sides at the stone strip halfway along where a door once stood. There is light coming from the sitting room and the fire snaps with fresh wood. She knows the guest must have put down fresh wood because these days uMesis would find such a thing too difficult.

There is something about the importance of the silver car and the confident way the man is speaking that makes her pause on the stone strip. The man sounds like a character from the television: a lawyer, maybe, or one of those judges with a little hammer who likes to make everyone rise up.

'If I remember myself correctly, I would have wanted to eat that fish.'

'You were a gentle child,' says uMesis. 'Always wanting to —'

She can hardly hear what uMesis is saying, so she inches forward, making a dangerous floorboard creak. But at the same moment, the man laughs, suggesting there is something funny in a place that Beauty can't reach.

'Don't you mean always wanting to please you?'

And in that instant she knows who he is, this man who talks like a character on the television, speaking to an audience that is not allowed to speak. The realisation makes her step forward without thinking, causing another floorboard to creak.

There is no time to consider what any of this might mean, and there is no time to think of Grace, because already she is walking forward — the floorboard having betrayed her — and entering the room.

But she sees at once that she needn't have worried: neither of them has heard her. UMesis is sitting unusually upright and Looksmart is standing further off, deeper into the room, his back turned against them like he is alone.

It takes a while for him to turn to them when she and uMesis begin to speak.

'Did you find Richard?'

'Cha, Mesis. And I can't find Bheki.'

'Then you must carry on looking.'

Beauty tries to catch the eye of uMesis, to understand what is happening, and what might be expected of her. But it seems that nothing is expected of her: uMesis is speaking as though Beauty hardly exists.

'Beauty, usangikhumbula?'

He is facing her now, standing at his full height, asking her to inspect him, no doubt expecting her to approve of him. She sees that he is tall, like his mother. The people from this area are usually smaller, in her experience, and not so arrogant. Looksmart's mother was never popular, and neither was her son. They came to the farm when Looksmart's mother was pregnant, with a story of a father in prison for a thing barely breathed about. A rape or a murder. The kind of crime for which he was fortunate not to have been hanged. But she is not sure whether anyone ever got to the bottom of what actually happened, or didn't happen. All that was ever known of the crime was its bad smell, which seemed to follow the family around forever afterwards.

She gets the same feeling from him now that she gets whenever she thinks about Grace. Like the memory of her, he is a thing to be avoided. They both make her want to run from there and be sick. She finds she is staring hard at the floor – not out of respect, but in order to hide her thoughts from him, from both of them.

'I know you. You are Looksmart.'

She can feel him exploring her woman's body and finding her wanting. They never liked each other: she was always the little sister, the ugly one, never any higher than his hips.

'Is that all you have to say?' he asks. He turns to uMesis and adds, 'I think she's intimidated by my suit.'

'Thank you, Beauty,' uMesis says. 'You can go and look for Richard now.'

Beauty looks up at last, her gaze burning into the indifference of his shoulder. Had either of them looked at her now, they might have seen the knowledge inside her eyes, smouldering like a fire, but without any light in it. But they are both too attached to their own concerns to see anything else.

'Ngiyabonga, Mesis,' she says, and in silence she leaves the room.

Patricia

She has often wondered whether she would see him again. He was so present when he was present, and when he went it was like all the colour had faded from the world. She barely noticed the phenomenon at first. She was too upset with him. And anyway she had decided she could do without him. But then the lack slowly dawned on her: a greyness entering into everything. It was not so much that the colour had gone as much as the thing that shone inside colour itself.

She suspected his mother knew why Looksmart had left and where he had gone, but to her enquiries she simply muttered, shrugged and drifted off towards her next task.

A few years later — still smarting from Looksmart's ingratitude — she told John Ford that the young man's behaviour didn't bode well for the rest of the country. What she meant by this exactly was unclear, even to her. By then the country had just had its first democratic elections and the general mood was optimistic, but Patricia hadn't forgotten the unofficial war that had assailed their province in the years preceding it, where children were slaughtered in their sleep and whole villages burned to the ground.

As the years went by, Patricia learned to shelve the disappearance of Looksmart along with all those other items she had never properly understood. It was a crowded shelf even then, and the matter of Looksmart often felt like the least of it.

When his mother vanished around the turn of the millennium, Patricia was so busy trying to save the farm from ruin that she barely thought about it. As Beauty told her at the time: 'That family was always difficult, from start to finish.'

He is pacing about, jumpy with nerves, like one about to step on a stage or make a speech. She still wants to ask him where he lives, what work he's doing, what brought him here. And she wants to know what it is that permits him to be so rude. He seems to find himself impressive for behaving like this – and for calling her 'Madam' with such contempt. She – who is used to seeing only small people these days, like Beauty and Richard, and even John Ford – finds him almost too large to countenance. Yet he still seems such a boy: at any moment, she is expecting him to show her his homework.

'So how did you come to be such a success?'

'This isn't fancy dress, Madam. I didn't dress like this to please you.'

'I know that.'

He is still looking around the house with that strange hunger. It's impossible to know what he's thinking or what he might be looking for. All she can see is her familiar rubbish. All the boxes splayed open, undignified and exposed, a life disembowelled. The wooden Dunlop tennis racquet she had as a girl, its leather handle still shining with the memory of her hot young hands. She took it to a tennis camp once in Howick. A boy there led her behind a shed and made her take his sex – a scarlet root, so unabashed – into her mouth. Then there's the German saddle her father gave her for her sixteenth birthday, the pommel now cracked and the grey stuffing bursting out. And the collection of Everyman Classics she'd once been given by John Ford – never read – with brown leather binding that was so obviously plastic when you pressed your thumbnail hard into it.

'You've caught us at quite a moment. If you'd come here tomorrow, I'm afraid you'd have found us gone.'

'You've sold the farm and are leaving tomorrow. I know all about that.'

'You do?'

'It's my business these days to know about such things.'

He turns to look at her. Then he steps towards her, again like a performer for the stage. A hypnotist? Certainly a charlatan of sorts.

'There's a secret network that runs underground. When it pleases me, I put my ear to it.'

'How mysterious that sounds.'

'It's no mystery.'

She wonders whether she should be afraid of him. There is certainly something dangerous about him – more the boy in him than the man. But in order to be afraid, one must have a thing of value that is under threat. And what is of value, after all? There is little difference, it seems to her, between herself and that tennis racquet.

Yesterday's blood: that is what is running through her body. The phrase came to her a few days previously – or at least, the thought did. To spill such blood would be to spill the blood of something already finished, or finished in all the ways that mattered. The only thing she has to look forward to these days is the house in Durban, which she sometimes suspects will vanish, like a rainbow, as soon as she reaches out to touch it.

But if fear is still far off, what she experiences in its place is a vacant sadness: that she and the boy with the fishing rod should have come to this.

'Tell me your plans,' he says, in a way that almost suggests he has been reading each of her thoughts.

'Me? Well, I'm going back to where I grew up. To my old house. By the sea.'

'Your father is dead?'

'Oh, for about fifty years now.'

Her father was dead when Looksmart was born, but she doesn't mention this. Instead she tells him that the house has been in her family for several generations, since her great-grandfather arrived in Durban. The city was said to be little more than a harbour back then, and Looksmart's ancestors were still living in the Valley of a Thousand Hills.

He doesn't appear to mind her talking. He seems to enjoy the sound of her voice – or perhaps there is a thing between her words that he can hear that she is unaware of. It unsettles her, the way he is listening and not listening. But then he surprises her again with his next question, which suggests he has been listening to her very closely after all.

'Won't you be sad to leave this place?'

'Oh, backward glances only crick the neck.'

He looks at her oddly, almost smiling, as he might at an exhibit in a museum.

'Sometimes a crick in the neck is exactly what the doctor orders.'

'Not at my age.'

He looks surprised by this statement: perhaps her age has never been an issue for him, or she has no age for him at all.

'But what will you do?'

'As little as possible. I plan to spend whole days simply looking at the sea.'

The ships will be there exactly as she recalls them, queuing across the horizon, honking as they come into the harbour. The thick wet salty air and the smell of rotten fruit. Everything shimmered in Durban with the sound of insects. There were birds in every tree, a flare of crimson wings as the louries flicked from branch to branch, and the emerald sunbirds as numerous as bees. She inherited a love of birds from her father. He taught her to identify every bird's egg and every call. She even tried to teach Richard the different birds in their early years – but he got no further than the yellow-billed duck.

'Have you ever heard the fruit bats?'

'In Durban? No, Madam. I can't say that I have.'

'They ping.'

'Ping?'

'They're as big as turtle doves. Someone once told me that they're the only bats the human ear can actually hear. They only come out at night, flapping around the stoep.'

It was her father who told her about the fruit bats – as the creatures passed back and forth through the veranda's light on their tattered wings. How she has since longed for them: that pulse in the trees, as if the whole hill is breathing.

'I remember that place as if I left it only yesterday.'

The thought of the house in Durban always used to make her blood sing, and she hopes the house will make it sing again. She may even be able to take up where she left off the day Richard arrived, and repair something, restore a vital ingredient, before she went away again for good.

'You'll think me foolish, Looksmart, but when you grow older, childhood things can seem magical.'

'Come, come, Madam. In my head, I can't separate you from this farm.'

'Over the years I might have settled here, grown into it. These days I'm so overgrown with creepers and moss, with old man's beard, that I probably look a part of it. But no – originally, I didn't actually come from these parts.'

He looks at her and shrugs. Whether she calls this place her home or not is clearly of no importance to him – or is perhaps hardly the point.

'What about the big Baas Richard? Won't he miss this place?'

'Richard? Well, he isn't well.'

'Not well, hey?' Looksmart looks delighted for a moment. 'What is it? A heart attack?'

'He's losing his mind. I mean – quite literally losing it.'

'And it's too late to find it?'

'Far too late to find it.'

They had always had this tone about Richard, which was designed to suggest they shared some joke about him. Yet it was a joke they never quite got around to sharing – Richard generally being a subject better laid to rest.

'It doesn't sound very jolly.'

'Oh, getting old rarely is.'

'But you've sold the farm. You must be rich.'

'We've been buried in debt for about as long as I can even – think. You know, for every rand the Welsh ponies brought in, Richard's cows and chickens cost another two. And Llewellyn died. You remember Llewellyn?'

He shrugs – perhaps in order to suggest that in his world a horse is of no real consequence. But she suspects he recalls Llewellyn well. In fact, there was once a picture of him in this very room, near the mantelpiece. When it fell down and the glass cracked and dropped out, they never got around to fixing it. She found the picture behind a sofa during the clearing up. The image was covered with a fine green fuzz of mould, and she binned it in a rubbish bag quickly, before she could dwell on it.

'Llewellyn was our very first stallion. All the foals came from him.'

Looksmart nods, unconsciously looking across at where the picture once hung. Although she might have planted his look there by looking there herself: maybe Looksmart really has no memory of the horse at all.

'When Llewellyn went, my interest in the stud seemed to fade. We sold the rest of the ponies off to a young man from White River. A man who looked very much like yourself. But Richard and I – we can't complain.'

'That's more than can be said for most of us.'

She lets out an involuntary and exasperated sigh.

'You don't look as if you've done too badly for yourself.'

'I don't?'

'And everyone has something or other they can choose to complain about.'

'Like what?' he says, again all ironic. 'Like getting old? Like being rich?'

She turns away, wishing he would leave, understanding that – for a while at least – he won't.

'I don't know what you're doing here,' she says. 'You have a whole future ahead of you. Why concern yourself with me and Richard? We are nothing in the world. We are practically antique.'

'What are you saying? That the past is unimportant?'

He sounds offended, and she recalls then how easily offended he often was. When he was hurt, he always wanted to draw a line between himself and others, and after he felt a bit better, he acted all surprised when there was no one around to take up his cause.

'Unimportant?' she says. 'I have no idea – but the past doesn't amount to much in the end, does it?'

She has been driving down the same dirt road for a long time now. There is sand in her hair and she needs a good wash. Some time back, many years it must have been, she turned a corner, turned it as she would have any other corner, but at that moment everything she'd thought about herself got lost. It would have been a fairly commonplace corner as she didn't even notice the event, but ever since then she has come to think of herself as some other woman, in some other woman's car.

He is staring at her with incomprehension, disbelief, and she wonders, not for the first time, whether she has been speaking her thoughts out loud. It was probably a thing that came from spending so many of her waking hours with Richard.

'Sorry, did I say something – inappropriate?'

'There's no need to apologise, Madam.'

'Apologise? But – I don't think I did.'

Richard

There is a light at the far end of the path and out of it comes the body of a woman, a small figure stepping out of heaven, at once known but not known. He wants to call her Mother, even though he knows that is not the right name for her. He wants to run to her and ask her his questions: where did the farm go? – for a start – and what am I expected to do about it? But he knows that she will pull him back towards the house where the bitch sits waiting, and so he would rather be here in the dark, trying to work everything out for himself.

Baas!

She is calling.

Or is he imagining this?

Ukuphi?

He slides down into what feels like a trench, his feet entering coolness and wet. There is a thornbush of barbed wire ahead of him, so he goes off in the other direction, away from the house, wishing for a moment that he had a gun.

But then what good is a gun against the dead?

Baas!

The phantom woman has veered off along another pathway, and he pauses as a runnel of warmness spreads down his legs. He does that at times: pisses without warning. It is a thing that happens of its own accord – the workings of his body being someone else's department.

There is too much to keep track of – that's the problem. The farm seems to have fallen apart completely in his absence, the land reduced to a bog, cows wandering about, swollen with milk, and stray chickens. And wasn't there even a donkey once? Now all the animals have nowhere to go: the fields ploughed up, the roads erased and all the buildings demolished. Although he wants to blame the bitch for all of this, he knows in his blood that it is more likely his fault. He has never been consistent. He can start off well enough, but everything soon gets broken down into bits. He can't piece together. For example, the spade. What did that have to do with this? It's another thing he let slip. The spade and what to do with it. There is something very important he came here to do but he. He doesn't know what.

Baas!

The voice has gone. That was only an echo. He peers over the edge and back into the world. And indeed the woman appears to have gone off again.

Was that his mom?

Rachel.

The spade.

But the earth is soft: he doesn't need a spade.

He will dig her up like a dog.

Beauty

Bheki is standing in one of the half-built houses. There is nothing but a floor, with walls beginning to grow out of the mud, and here and there the suggestion of a window or doorframe. Where uMesis likes to sit in the front room, a big bonfire burns, making it look like uMesis has just been set on fire. Beauty can't help but feel that the placement of the fire is intended. A ritual of some kind is being performed. If not on uMesis herself then on the idea of uMesis. But this is a crazy thought, as the men who made the fire – the builders – have only ever seen uMesis in the distance and have never set foot in her house. As for Bheki, he would have no need to burn uMesis: he cares about her – and he cares for her – almost as much as Beauty does.

Dead Oudehout branches from the indigenous forest above the marsh have been dragged here to feed the flames. There are also branches of the tree with leaves of silver velvet and there's a thick yellowwood branch twisting and crackling. The use of the yellowwood is disturbing, as this is a sacred, slow-growing tree that would never usually be used for firewood. She wonders how Bheki could have permitted this act of disrespect. But when she considers reprimanding the builders herself, she understands that she and Bheki have no hold over the farm any more: by this time tomorrow, they will be gone and the builders will be able to do whatever they like.

There are several other men standing around the bonfire. Their shapes lurch from side to side as the fire adjusts itself to the weather. There is more mist than rain now, and it makes the air glow a dirty orange around them. Bheki is standing with his back to her, looking smaller than before. A drab waterbird hunched in the rain. An old blanket, looking like a pair of broken wings, hangs from his shoulders.

The other men are stamping their feet for warmth, murmuring and looking satisfied with themselves. She knows Bheki doesn't fit with them, even if he's pretending he does. It is one of the things she loves about Bheki: his awkwardness amongst others, and the privacy he carries with him, even in the presence of uMesis or uBaas. If there were ancestors, they would have chosen Bheki as the best father for that cuckoo-boy with the blue eyes: they would have known that such a man would be up to the task of loving the boy, and of understanding that the boy is no different from anyone else.

Yet here he is, amongst these men whose names he hardly knows. Men have always been incomprehensible to her. The way they come together like this and assume a hardness and a looseness that they never have when standing alone. She wonders whether she would like them better if she saw them as she sees Bheki, but she doubts it. She can't accept the ease with which men dispense with themselves and become something else, which would suggest that nothing matters to them in the end but fitting in for the moment. Yet Bheki is apparently no different either: he also chooses to stand here at the fire, getting lost in the other men, like a savage preparing himself to go into a battle without a name.

'Bheki, uphi uBaas?'

She can feel that he doesn't want to be tracked down like this. It is his last night on the farm and he has chosen to be here, hidden amongst these men. She knows he doesn't care for them, but that is exactly why he is here: here he can stand and turn over each of his slow thoughts without anyone even touching him.

'Cha.'

It is also embarrassing for him to be sought out over such a question. Have you seen uBaas? Like he is a woman, a nurse, whose job is to run around after a mad umlungu. The other men will be thinking: that is what this man's life has amounted to.

'Ulahlekile,' he says, spitting into the flames in a way that suggests the old man has always been lost.

She is not surprised by this treatment. It's what men do. They treat women differently when they are with other men. No, that is not true: they treat women like Beauty differently when they are with other men. Those women who can be laughed off. Those women who stand alone in the world because they are not attractive to any man with eyes, with standards.

Normally, she would have faded back into the night, leaving Bheki with his thoughts, and forgetting the other men instantly – as the problem of other women. But tonight she needs Bheki. She knows uMesis and Looksmart can't be left alone in the house. Some dark event is hurtling towards them, like a train coming through the night, aimed straight for the house. She knows why Looksmart is here. She knows better than even Looksmart does. And she knows the one thing she needs to achieve is to keep away uBaas.

'Kunendoda endlini,' she continues. 'Ngidinga ukukhuluma nawe.'

When Bheki hears the tone in her voice, he does not fight against it. He throws something into the fire – a spent thought or a cigarette – and walks towards her, stepping through the place where the front window will be and onto what will soon become the stoep.

'Indoda?'

'ULooksmart. Uyamkhumbula?'

It is clear that Bheki remembers him, as he remembers everything. He asks what Looksmart wants.

'Angazi. Usendlini noMesis. Yingakho ngidinga usizo ukuthola uBaas.'

She can feel the hesitation inside Bheki. Every day, each of them has to make a fresh decision to look out for uBaas. The decision is never made for uBaas's sake but for the sake of another thing: the expectations of uMesis, or the protection of a job.

'Angaba noma kuphi.'

She tells Bheki to look in all the usual places. She repeats the same list of uMesis: the dairy buildings, the chicken shed, the fields where the last remaining cows used to graze, the grave on the hill.

'Uyabona-ke kungani kumele ngimlethe endlini?'

'Mlethe endlini la esihlala khona.'

'Ngoba?'

She can't tell him exactly why uBaas must be taken back to her room and kept away from the house. Right now, the reason feels too big for her to be able to explain it.

'Ngoba?' he asks again.

But already she has turned away from him – and the men standing mute around the fire – and is trotting back towards the house.

Looksmart

All of this was far easier to think about when he wasn't here, facing her, having to endure her presence, her gestures – let alone the words she has chosen for herself. He wishes for some of his old hate, which never paused to think, but he knows that he will have to try a different path towards her, one that is more subtle, more accurate, more effective in the end.

'What I find interesting is this idea you have,' he says, 'that the past is – what was it – unimportant?'

'I don't think I ever said that.'

'Because that suggests to me that there are no consequences to people's actions, and I find that idea, I find it repugnant.'

'That's a strong word, Looksmart.'

It is easy to say the words of hate. He can reproduce them automatically, and fool her into thinking he still knows what it is to hate. But he also knows that with these words can come hate itself, stepping in through the back door – as he did, into the house.

'Are you saying you have a clear conscience about the past?'

She looks at him with apparent incomprehension, perhaps bordering on fear. Does she think he is speaking generally? She seems to have no idea of what he means specifically, but then she's never been much good at interrogating herself.

He remembers her well back then: how she liked to live with her head buried deep in the earth, while the rest of the country was in flames, with bombs going off in Johannesburg, and the so-called faction fighting all around them in Natal. Back then, all she seemed to want to talk about was the farm and him. On occasions it even sounded like she wanted him to compensate for the farm's failure: he was expected to provide fresh prospects and a steely ambition. But he was growing too complicated even to himself by then ever to be able to satisfy her.

'Few of us can say they have a conscience about the past,' she says. 'I doubt such a thing exists.'

She was always cleverer than he, even when he was the cleverest boy at that very clever school. She had cleverness in her blood. She never needed to open a book or make an effort to think. Her head was already in the clouds anyway, and her thoughts came down to him – to all of them – like sharp little swallows diving down from the sun.

'How easily you let yourself off the hook.'

'What hook?'

She might be cleverer, but he knows he has a far better memory than she: for while she was in the clouds, he has been on the ground, living amongst the rest of humanity, knowing all along how her particular kind of cleverness diminished them.

So naturally he remembers that day they went to fish. It was a thing that was impossible to forget: him learning to cast on the front lawn, weaving the line back and forth through the air, back and forth, and her perched up there on her stoep, ordering him about and laughing at him like he was her toy, her toy monkey, with a battery up its arse.

All the time, he was just trying to get it right. All he ever wanted was to impress her, to show how he wasn't like the rest of them – the natives – who had to be told a hundred times how to do a thing before they could master it.

'You know,' he says, 'I think I do remember that first fish. But what I remember is the rock. You gave me a rock to smack its head. I had to hit its head with a rock.'

It seems to take her a while to bring her thoughts back down to his, and to recollect the business of the fish, and who did what when – as if any of it actually mattered to her.

'I think you're thinking of another occasion,' she says. 'Some other fish. And anyway, isn't that what you're supposed to do? You have to kill a fish quickly. To put it out of its misery.'

He hears himself laughing. It is the kind of laughter designed to suggest he feels nothing for her, and nothing for putting her out of her misery – or into the very heart of it.

Perhaps, after all, he really will be able to regain his hate.

'All I'm saying, Madam, is that I think we do far too much of this – letting people off the hook. You see, I'm a far more effective fisherman now.'

As he passes the apple and the wooden-handled fruit knife, he picks up the apple – and then, almost as an afterthought, the knife. The apple he tosses into the air and catches, doing this a few times, as one would a cricket ball on a Sunday afternoon – like someone about to bowl, his family eating sandwiches from behind the boundary line, instead of working in the fields, knee-deep in shit.

'You make that sound almost like a threat.'

He can see that she still isn't sufficiently afraid of him.

'A threat? I do? Well,' he says, 'I'd have to think very carefully about that one.'

He hears the same hard laughter coming out of him. It is a sound his daughters would not recognise. It is a laugh that comes from before. It is a thing he learned here. It is of this place, not the present. The present right now seems very remote from him.

'One could argue that it wouldn't be in my interests to threaten you.'

'Quite.'

'One could point out my wife, my daughters, and my well-paying job. Do you know that your garden boy is now driving a Mercedes-Benz?'

She looks at him with wonder, quite the opposite of impressed. But he knows what he is doing far better than she thinks. With every sentence, he is cutting down any claims of affection that might stand, like so many weeds, between them. For his whole life, it seems to him, he has been circumnavigating her sensitivities. Even after he left her, her gaze was still fixed upon him.

'These days,' he is saying, 'I am indeed what people like to call a success. Do you want to know how much I paid for this suit?'

'I couldn't care less what you paid for that suit.'

'Of course, you would have forgotten what a car right out of the box looks like, or smells like. The freshly stitched leather, the air of wealth that breathes out of the air conditioner. My car is like a racehorse – skittish, responding to my every thought, my lightest touch. But you wouldn't know anything about that. Not these days. What with that wreck of yours still sitting there under its tin roof.'

Like a fat toad, he wants to add, at the heart of his life.

When he has finished this speech, he has to sit down on a trunk. On the wall in front of him, the plaster has fallen away to reveal the dark grey stone – yet he barely registers this.

'I don't know what's got into you, Looksmart. You can't come into people's houses and start – talking like this.'

'I can't?' he says, trying to sound both dumb and ironic.

'What is it that you want?'

'Patience,' he says, as much to himself as to her. 'Patience is rewarded at the end to those who wait.'

Even his language, he is pleased to discover, is slipping away from him. All the old errors he used to make in her company are coming back to him, like long-lost friends. He welcomes them: each one tells her how he has shrugged off her good advice and chosen a different path, one that is indifferent to getting her language right. And it doesn't even matter that this isn't true.

'My husband will soon be getting back,' she says, looking more frightened of him at last – now that he is losing the ability to speak.

'From what?'

But his assumed ease is nothing more than a front: behind it, he is trying to think, trying to understand where all of this is leading them and what he ought to do next. He is also well aware of the old Baas's absurd collection of guns somewhere inside the house. They used to sit in his study inside a glass case, during the days when you still displayed your guns, when such a display might have warned people off – whereas these days they are to the tsotsis like sweets in a shop window.

So he starts to peel away at the fruit, the waxy skin dropping down into a perfect spiral. No harm can come to him, he tells himself, for what harm has he done? He resembles nothing more than a man in a suit, peeling a piece of fruit at his leisure – while that woman sits there, angled against her chair as if it's hurting her.

'I'm not sure who you are any more,' she tells him.

'Oh, people change,' he says. 'That is certainly true. Wouldn't you say that's true of you?'

She is staring at him with that white person's look, blank and faintly beaming, while inside she contemplates her long row of denigrating thoughts about him. He knows the look well enough. It is something he learned to do himself from her, although he never had the courage to direct it back to where it came from.

'Everything's changed, hasn't it?' she says. 'The country – the country and everything that's in it.'

'And you are pleased about that?'

'Oh, my opinion hardly counts,' she says, in a way that suggests her opinion is the only thing that has ever mattered – at least to anyone with any sense.

'Don't worry, Madam. I am very interested in what goes on between your ears.'

She is watching the coupling of the apple and the knife from far off, as one might watch a snake in the hands of an expert. For now, it seems, she has chosen to trust the handler, or otherwise that's what she wants the handler to think.

'Are you afraid?' he asks her.

'Is that what you're after?'

He doesn't answer this, but he realises that it is indeed what he's after, or at least some part of him. He has come here to witness the resurgence of his hatred and her fear, and he is prepared to wait up all night if that's what it takes.

'What exactly do you want me to be afraid about?'

'What you have always been afraid about: the truth.'

'The truth?'

She says this as though the truth is a concept only children believe in, like dragons and houses made out of bread and cake.

Patricia

Of course, there is much to be afraid about. She has long ago given up reading the newspapers or watching the news: it was always the same story, even if the names were slightly different. But there are times when the stories happen so near to her that she can't avoid them. Only a week ago, a friend from a nearby farm, a woman she hadn't seen for several years now, was tied up with wire and raped, and then her throat was cut. Or perhaps her throat was cut and then she was raped: it was not clear which happened first.

Her name was Fiona Johnson. She and Patricia were at boarding school together in Hilton. Back then, Fiona was a swimmer and gymnast, with lovely long brown legs that she wanted every boy to notice. Her legs would enter the room first, and Fiona would appear soon afterwards, usually with a broad smile on her face. Later, she married a polocrosse player who ran a stud for Arabs. They had three girls with the same legs as their mother, who went to the same school and then faded from Patricia's view. While the husband was away, Fiona's attackers entered the house at dusk, during a thunderstorm. They tied her up like a bale of hay and slaughtered her like a sheep: it was a good farm murder.

'I'm afraid you're not even a shadow of the little boy I knew.'

'I was hardly a little boy, Madam. I was what? Nineteen when I left?'

'You think at nineteen you're a man? Is that what you think?'

'I was a man. You made me to be a man.'

'Well that's something, isn't it?'

'You don't know what I mean.'

'How can I? You're being so – perverse.'

'You think I'm a pervert?'

'That's not what I said!'

She doesn't know what might have happened to his English. In the circles he moves these days there's probably no need for good English. All she knows is that he spoke far better as a child.

Looksmart

He places the apple very deliberately on the mantelpiece, the apple and its afterthought of skin. The knife he closes and slips into his pocket. It is frightening, horrible, alluring: the thought that a man in his position might decide to kill her.

'Do you remember those clay animals I made you once?'

'Hmm?'

Only now has he recollected that misplaced menagerie, arranged all along that shelf. His mother had spoken of a stream up on the mountain where you could find good clay. She said you had to shove away the darker mud to reach it. So he and another boy went up there and arrived at it: a meagre spring that gurgled out of the earth. A malachite sunbird was nesting above it, like a blessing. At first they contented themselves with flicking the clay at each other from the ends of wattle sticks. Then they took some back to the compound and made miniature soldiers, which were a dull hard grey by the following morning.

Looksmart returned weeks later, in secret, to see what else he could make. He started off moulding a cow and ended up with a figure from his dreams that had a human body and an antelope head. The next day he was pleased to find his small imaginings still standing there, consolidated into stone. He didn't know what else to do but take them to show her.

'You must remember,' he says. 'I made them when I was still a boy. About the time I started to come to your house.'

'Yes, yes of course I do.'

'Yes. Yes of course you do.'

He finds he doesn't believe her. Right now she would say anything to make him go away again.

'I was so proud when you put them up there,' he says, 'on your mantel-piece. Whenever I came into this room, I would look to see if they were still there – in place.'

He sees them dawning on her now, marching one by imperfected one back into her consciousness – or is it merely the idea of them she seems to like?

'After a while,' he says, 'they seemed to knock into each other, crack up. There was a dislodged head, a broken ear, an animal with its legs snapped off, lying upside-down on its back.'

He is making much of this up. All he can recall is bringing them to her in his shirt and watching her placing them along the shelf, and congratulating him – the toy monkey with the battery up its arse.

'And then one day, they were gone.'

They both wait for a while, as if expecting the clay creatures to reappear. But nothing happens: the tin roof ticks as raindrops are released from a tree above it: the wind is starting up. Outside, he sees it is unambiguously dark. The windows are a black mirror in which they move, deep underwater.

'You had talent. Are you still doing any art?'

His old laughter once again comes back at him, like a sickness, like whooping cough.

'Art? I was only trying to impress you. You call that art?'

'You had something – magical in your touch.'

This sounds like a declaration of love, unexpected and almost embarrassing. He sees that she is watching him in an older way now. Perhaps she is finally beginning to find traces of the boy he once was in him – but this is a thing he must guard himself against if he's to make any progress here at all.

'I wonder where Richard is,' she now says, when the air between them has slightly cooled. But there's also a note of accusation in her voice: perhaps she suspects him of harming the old Baas, of leaving him dead in a ditch.

'Well, I might have – bumped into him,' he concedes.

But he is thinking – as he says this – that there must be something wrong with her: to have been able to share her life with a man like that, let alone her bed. When she says nothing further, he adds: 'There are so many men in the world, Madam. Why did you have to choose that one?'

But she doesn't answer this either: about her husband she has always been far too reticent.

'Aren't you going to offer me some tea?' he says abruptly – surprising them both. 'Tea and carrot cake. Isn't that what you usually offer to your guests?'

'It's a bit too late for tea, don't you think?'

Even though she might not be frightened enough, he can see that she can still be offended, hurt: by disregarding the proper time for tea, he is by implication disregarding her.

'If you insist.'

He tells her by his silence that he does indeed insist.

'Although I'm afraid we don't have any cake,' she adds. 'Tea we have, tea and I think some Marie biscuits.'

'Thank you, Madam. That would be nice.'

They both wait, as if expecting – by some miracle – Beauty to appear. But she doesn't appear, and it seems Patricia can't easily get up to find her. Since his arrival, she has been stuck to that chair, and he has wondered before whether or not she's lost the ability to walk.

'Beauty!'

Then he understands: she doesn't want to call the girl in front of him: this time, she didn't call out the name in her usual way, which is almost sung, the second syllable far higher than the first. No – she called her as she might have called a sister, or a friend.

'Try it again, Madam.'

'Sorry?'

'That is not how it's usually done.'

'What are you talking about?'

It is clear she knows exactly what he is talking about.

'She won't come unless you call her like you're calling one of your dogs.'

'How dare you speak to me like —'

'Like what?' he almost laughs. 'Like a dog?'

She stares deep into the fire, which has been reduced to glowing embers, but they are pulsing now as though a current is being fed directly from her into them.

'Come on, Madam. Try it.'

'I will not.'

'Try it again. For old time's sake.'

Patricia

'Beau-ty!'

Beauty

UMesis is sitting far back in her chair, her head to one side, as she does whenever she has taken too many pills for her pain. She doesn't turn to look at Beauty. She is staring towards a thing not visible in the room. She looks like one of those plump baby pigeons preparing to leave the nest: fluffy and grotesque, with a watchful intensity, but also subsided into itself, knowing it will never be capable of flight.

'Mesis?'

'Beauty,' she says without stirring. 'Yes. Have you found Richard yet?'

The way uMesis says this suggests they will never be able to find uBaas again. It is as bad as that, the way she says it.

'Mesis, I have not found him.'

She tries to speak in her usual way – in order to reassure uMesis that uBaas will be found and brought back to the house in the usual way. But it is clearer than ever that if uBaas is still out there, he must be kept as far away from the house as possible.

'And Bheki?'

'Mesis?'

'Did you ask Bheki to look for him?'

'Yebo, Mesis. And I know Bheki can find him soon.'

UMesis doesn't react to this. Perhaps she has already given up hope. Beauty feels an impulse to go up to uMesis and shake her, or slap her hard across the face. Yet, as ever, she is powerless to step in, to intervene.

'What about the tea?'

It is Looksmart who says this. He has that same mesmerised look as uMesis, but it is not that of the bird, it is more the look of its predator.

'Oh yes,' uMesis says. 'I was wondering if you could bring in some tea. And also the Marie biscuits.'

'The biscuits, they have gone soft, Mesis.'

'Then put them in the oven. Dry them out.'

Looksmart

How little they have advanced, the numberless dispossessed. He sees them every day in the streets of Johannesburg, standing at traffic lights with signs around their necks, mimicking disability or blindness, kneeling in the middle of the road in the rain, wearing layers of rubbish bags for clothes, their hair like wire wool that has been used to scour a burned frying pan, all for two coins that they can rub together to buy bread, or some glue to sniff.

The tribe of Beauty is not so different – living in their huts throughout these hills, with a bucket to wash from and a pot to eat from, and often little else. If they are lucky, they will have a bicycle and a walkie-talkie for keeping in touch with the big Baas up in the main house.

When he first started to earn a decent salary, Looksmart had a collection of silver coins in his car for the poor. He prided himself on always giving something. He liked to touch the leathery outstretched palms with his fingers as the devout in Europe are said to touch the hands or feet of bronze saints. The coin he offered up to appease his guilt was like collection during chapel, a practice he used to observe with mute wonder at boarding school, since the money forever seemed to him to be passing between the wrong people. But more recently he has stopped giving anything to beggars. At the traffic lights, he stares ahead, too preoccupied to see them, until the cars ahead have moved on.

'She hasn't changed.'

'Beauty?'

Patricia says this with some complacency, possibly to suggest it is a good thing for people like Beauty not to change – a good thing for Beauty as much as for her employers.

'She keeps herself to herself.'

'And she has never had any children?'

'She says she doesn't want any.'

'And you believe that?'

'I've never had any reason not to.'

'But what about a husband?'

'She says she isn't interested in men either.'

'I wonder why,' he says with some irony.

But it is a nascent anger he is beginning to feel concerning Beauty – not pity. What did the girl expect by staying on in this place, especially after what had happened to Grace? To remain on the farm was to condone what had happened here – and that was one thing he himself was never prepared to do. At the time, of course, Beauty can't have been older than thirteen, but she has had a good twenty-five years since that moment to develop some self-respect.

'Beauty and Bheki will be coming with us to Durban tomorrow.'

'Well, isn't that nice.'

The old woman barely looks at him, however: she appears to be growing tired of his techniques.

'I suppose I knew her older sister better,' Looksmart continues, trying to keep his voice level. 'You remember her older sister? Her name was Grace.'

'Grace?'

'Yebo, Madam. Grace. A lot like Beauty, only far more beautiful.'

She seems to sense the change in him, and leans forward slightly in her chair, as if she has caught the scent of something animal in the air. She can't yet know that it is his old rage, his old hate — which, at the mention of Grace's name, has finally arrived in the room in a way it hadn't yet managed before. But Looksmart recognises it at once: it floods his blood with a morbid ecstasy.

'Of course I know who Grace was,' she prattles on. 'She was the girl from the dairy who died.'

'Who died or was killed, Madam?'

He almost whispers this, but every syllable is deliberate and clear. The way he asks it is intended to be as shocking as the question itself. When she says nothing, he adds: 'You do not like the distinction?'

'I'm afraid I have absolutely no idea what you're talking about,' she says — an involuntary shudder betraying her.

'At the time, I saw it as murder, plain and simple.'

'Murder?'

'Mur-der.'

She lets out a sigh of exasperation and falls, deflated, back into her chair. But he can see it is all an act: she is trying to buy time, her embattled brain racing with thoughts, her eyes darting back and forth, as if to catch up with the flickering images crowding in on her.

'Looksmart, I really don't know what's got into you,' she says, still no doubt biding her time, 'but the boy I knew, he would never have been able to — to come in here and speak like this.'

'You never knew me, Madam!' he says — with more venom than she would ever have heard from him before. 'Looksmart! What was that? You don't even know my name!'

'It's Looksmart, of course.'

'That is not my name.'

'But I was there when you were born,' she practically shouts. 'I remember the exact moment your mother named you Looksmart!'

Three

Patricia

It was a wet night like this. She was sitting alone in her chair, staring at the television, when there was a rattle at the front door. She thought it was the wind, but when she went there, she found one of the workers. He said the baby was on its way: she should come.

She didn't know where Richard was. He was probably out with the latest stable girl from England, in a pub deep in the hills, sitting by a fire, their knees touching under the table while they talked about England and all the things they missed: the weather, greasy spoons, public transport, unemployment, Margaret Thatcher. The truth was that she gave neither Richard nor England any thought as she put on her coat and left the house.

The wind was huge in the bloodwoods and the rain was soon stinging their faces, but she — flanked by the dogs — followed the man down to the compound, her feet finding their way in the darkness.

She had attended many births. Mainly horses, cattle and sheep. She had even been present, to some extent, at the birth of Rachel. But each time the characters and the story that unfolded between them was different. Every mother was different and went through so many different states that it was impossible by the end to say much about the birth that felt sufficient. It was a good birth, a bad birth – these hardly went anywhere in describing it.

What never differed, however, was the contrast between the mother and all those around her. Everyone was helpless, exhausted, apologetic, but the observers always stood on the periphery, while the mother provided the heart of the storm. The mother sat at the place that couldn't be climbed away from, yet every mother at a certain point tried to get out of the bed, and get away from the birth, the pain of it. Yet every mother was thrown back down and subjected to the event, which had been painful, according to the Bible, since the moment Eve had tasted that apple and brought upon humanity God's hideous curse.

The baby came from far away, and the mother was lying on the shore, amongst the broken waves, heaved about, this way and that – and the new life was distant at first, on the other side of the waves, far out to sea, little more than a boat bobbing, almost beyond sight – and each new wave became a contraction, twisting through the woman's body, pulling the small boat closer.

'Iminjunju le.'

That is what Looksmart's mother said to Patricia when she entered the dimly lit hut.

Then she said in English, 'I am pain.'

Every part of her body looked twisted up like a wet towel. She was struggling to take off her necklace because she couldn't breathe. Not long afterwards, during a contraction, her waters broke and she let out a moan of sorrow.

'I can't get the baby out. It is stuck.'

'It isn't stuck.'

Patricia was saying this.

'The pain is your friend. It is there to help get the baby out.'

Every mother had to find that moment when they changed their minds about the pain, when it was a thing they no longer tried to escape, but became something they started to use, to work with, riding through it, not stopping at it – using it not as obstacle, but as a horse.

'Don't scream. You're wasting energy. Instead, you must push.'

It took another hour of screaming and not screaming before the baby came out, grey and wet and rubbery, like a big dead fish. But it wasn't dead. Patricia lifted it up and it took its first breath – and screamed. And everyone, except the mother, laughed. The mother was too far away, too emptied out, reduced to a husk.

Patricia knew at once that there was nothing weak about this baby. They cut the cord and it screamed again and they knew it was going to be all right. The baby was wrapped in a bundle and handed to the mother and immediately he found her nipple and started to suck. Even though her milk hadn't arrived yet, he knew what he was about – what he wanted and where it would come from. He was never going to apologise to anyone.

'A strong little chap, that's what he will be,' Patricia said.

'We will call him Looksmart,' said his mother.

Usually, Patricia would have left, but that night she sat by the bed, waiting to make sure the mother and child would be all right – and waiting to see if they would be able to sleep. But the mother didn't sleep, only the baby did. And when he was asleep, holding onto her breast like he had always been there, the mother drank a mug of sweet tea and Patricia drank one with her. They stared at the tiny sleeping face for so long that all other faces looked impossibly huge, like exaggerated moons.

It was a good night to be born. The gentle rain nourishing the earth. The earth's wetness went deep and everything was washed clean. It felt, for an hour or two, that nothing wicked would ever be left in the world.

Every day after that Patricia would go down to the hut to look at the child. He would stare deep into her eyes, stare as though he was still that small boat beyond the waves and was still trying to arrive.

'Who are you?' she would ask him.

'Who are you?' his eyes would answer back.

He moved like an underwater creature. His body still carried the memory of the womb. His little hands and feet were suspended, as if floating, without gravity.

She never told Richard about the newborn child. Children had become one of the topics they avoided. But it was more than that. She had found a place where Richard was not, where something altogether outside of him existed. She experienced her visits to the compound much as she would later experience her visits to Rawdons Hotel with John Ford: it was a secret pleasure and an act of defiance. Not so much against Richard as in the opposite direction from him, towards everything Richard was not — towards life.

Richard

He's never understood the workings of the house. The fact is it was never his house, but hers, handed down from her father. While he was there on good behaviour. Which is why he thinks he chose bad behaviour. Because too much good behaviour after a while feels like a lie that has to be broken. Even if the breaking is a lie, as well as everything that comes after to replace it.

But he has understood enough to know where the front gate is. He'll give himself that. And the stretch of the lawn to the point of the stoep, and the height of the roof against the whispering trees, and the surprising symmetry of the chimneys at either side. Always there has been the light coming from the room where she likes to sit, summoning up some nasty thought to direct at him.

So he finds he is not prepared for this. The driveway gone, blown to bits, and a mound of earth the size of an elephant exactly where the gate is meant to be. He ascends the mound to find the house, which takes longer than expected because the top half of it has been removed. Only those parts most fastened to the earth have managed to stick.

Help me.

He says this or thinks it so as to remind himself of himself. But he is also afraid of being overheard. There will be a farmer inside that house, his house, who could take one look at the bog-man on the mound and get his gun and have a shot at him. But if this is not his house, then where is his house?

No: he knows this has to be his house. There is enough of it still standing to recognise it. The only explanation left is that he is dead, and time has moved on, and while he was busy being dead, the farm and everything on it has fallen into ruin.

Help.

But there is another thing, almost worse. The house – or what is left of it – is filled with guests. Milling about, coming and going, arranged around a fire that looks too big for any fireplace to contain. He doesn't seem to recognise any of the guests. Most of them are wearing bright yellow jackets, but others wear black binbags and one or two a sack. They do not look like the kind of guests the old bitch would have welcomed into the house, which must mean that she is also gone, or otherwise dead – maybe even murdered and buried under one of these mounds.

He looks again at his boots and sees that they are two muddy clumps. They haven't been polished for years. Which confirms to him that the bitch is most undeniably dead.

Oh help.

He feels tired now. Tired of walking, tired of the rain, tired of being dead. Nobody will notice if he goes to his room, finds his bed, permits himself a few hours of rest. It's difficult to see in the dark and the rain, and when he fingers his face he finds his glasses are also gone. But it doesn't matter: he can feel his way back into the house. If he could only have one small sleep, he might wake up to find all of this shifted – or simply more warmth, if nothing else, and if he's lucky some light.

Then he has a better idea: he could have a shower, get drier shoes, track down that long-lost herringbone coat, and then go and help himself to a drink. Who's to say he isn't another guest? If he doesn't know these men, they won't know him. They won't know he once owned this place. Or that his wife did. And that he was once the one to stand in this house and order everyone about.

He slides down the elephant slope and wades through the grass where the lawn is meant to be. Here and there are outcrops of bricks, piled neatly, with a decorum he can appreciate. He encounters a water trough that resembles those from the paddocks – it's an old bath, half-filled with rainwater – and here he stops and drinks, his nostrils flaring. The water tastes familiar, like melted ice.

Perhaps it is the language he can overhear that puts him off, but he finds after he drinks that he doesn't trust these guests. The way they choose to live, for example. Without even a roof over their heads. He knows that if they saw him they would want to turn on him and hunt him down. They would want to beat him, kick him, throw him into the fire for sport. It would be better if he went to bed and waited for them to go back home. Then he could get through to the sitting room and drink up the dregs of beer and help himself to any leftover meat.

But when he arrives at his bedroom, he drops the brick he discovers in his hand: there is no window to smash. Instead he finds half a wall and a vacancy where the window is supposed to be. The room itself has been cleared out and all that is left is a wheelbarrow and a few sacks of cement. And what appears to be a familiar grey donkey, standing there in place of his bed, staring at him and chewing grass.

Beauty

Beauty turns off the gas and removes the biscuits from under the grill. They're looking slightly charred in places, but not so soft any more. By the time they reach uMesis, they will still be warm, like they have been freshly baked. But they are a sorry sight when she puts them on the plate. Far from the Madeira cake uMesis taught her to make, with its golden crust of lemony sugar and easily subsiding softness underneath. These look like something rescued from a house on fire.

But there is no time to dwell on this. The biscuits can still be a distraction from whatever is being said in that room. Even from here she can hear the voices. She is used to this feeling of having shouting in the house. This feeling of some dangerous thing being circled through words, or gradually taken apart. Tonight, however, it feels different: this is not the occupation of two bored people trying to argue their way back into feeling again: this is the sound of two people who are feeling too much.

'My name is Phiwayinkosi,' she can hear him saying. 'Phiwayinkosi Ndlovu. That is the name my parents gave me. Looksmart? That is only the name they gave in order to please you. But I am not here to talk about this. I am here to talk about Grace. The sister of Beauty. The girl I loved.'

'The girl you loved? But at the time I didn't know anything about that.'

'Well – you wouldn't have.'

She comes into the room before more can be said, and they both turn towards her as if expecting to see Grace herself: but all they find is the disappointment of Beauty.

'Nanti itiye, Mesis.'

She stands there as the bearer of the tea and a scattering of burned biscuits, nothing more. As there is no obvious place to put the tray, she balances it on a pile of boxes. It is not a position she would have chosen were there still dogs in the house, but this is a room where nothing much moves any more. She pours the tea in silence, surrounded by silence.

'Ngiyabonga, Beauty. Umtholile uBaas?'

'Cha, Mesis.'

'But Bheki is still looking?'

'Yebo, Mesis.'

'Don't worry,' says uMesis without much conviction, 'he always turns up in the end.'

Beauty hands uMesis her cup of tea but leaves the other cup alone on the tray, as she would for a guest who hasn't yet arrived. Then she turns towards the door.

'I'll have mine with milk – Togo.'

She has seldom been called by that other name since she was a girl. It takes her completely by surprise and wrenches something inside her. She has to stop and breathe before she can return to normal. When she meets his gaze at last, however, it is to tell him that she no longer recognises herself by that name. Then she goes back to the tray and pours the other cup of tea: first the milk, as uMesis has taught her, and then the tea. The excessive ritual of it is intended as a kind of insult, but then she sees that Looksmart is hardly watching her. She places the cup on a box near him, just beyond the reach of his arm, so that he will have to walk across to get it.

'And sugar,' he says. 'Three and a bit.'

Leaving the cup on its box, she brings the sugar bowl back to it. She knows this is not how it ought to be done, but she intends this as another kind of insult. She drops three piled spoons of the moist white sugar into the cup, forgetting his other 'bit', and declines to stir it. As she is turning away again, she notices the apple on the mantelpiece – its skin unravelled, as if the apple has tried to spin away from itself – and she wonders briefly where the knife has gone.

'Keep looking, Beauty,' uMesis says – and it takes a moment for Beauty to understand that she is still talking about uBaas.

Looksmart

'The big Baas Richard! When I think of him, I think of a soft, white moth: small, weak, without any blood. When I take him between my finger and my thumb to find out what is there, I find he has just turned to dust.'

An English teacher at school once said he could become a poet. Images seemed to fly down from the air around his head and settle on the page intact. But he felt even then that words were not to be trusted. There was nothing wrong with them in themselves, he supposed. They existed in books and in the mouths of people as naturally as pebbles along a dried-out river-bed. It was the way words were used in the world that made them, and those who relied too much on them, suspicious.

'Looksmart, I hope you aren't about to make a serious mistake.'

And then he understands: that is exactly what he has come here to do: to risk making a serious mistake. So far, he's hardly ever put a foot wrong – except, perhaps, for the odd deception to the taxman or his wife. But publicly he's been no less than a saint: everywhere he walks has been like holy ground, leading to profit, each step always an advancement on the one that came before. Well, he's grown tired of that. These days, his footsteps have developed a hollow ring to them, like the words in a sentence that is known to be a lie.

'I can see it all quite clearly,' he tells her.

'See what? What on earth are you talking about?'

'I want you to tell me everything – everything you remember about that girl Grace.'

'But it happened such a long time ago.'

They are sitting outside on the stoep. It is late afternoon. At any moment the horses will be brought to the front lawn to be presented, examined, corrected. Patricia's chair stands in its usual late afternoon sunbeam. And everything looks golden, the roses lit up, the wisteria fragrant in the eaves, the sunbirds chirruping – all that usual idyllic farmhouse crap – when they hear a faraway cry, coming from the direction of the dairy, sounding barely human.

And then silence.

'Did you never wonder why her clothing was in tatters?'

'Grace?'

He stares at her, full of contempt, waiting for her to speak.

'When we first saw her,' she says, 'she was – wasn't she half-dressed?'

Patricia was telling him to go and investigate that animal cry when they saw her, running along the dirt track that passes around the house.

'And you never wondered about that?'

'It was the police's job – to wonder about that.'

He sits down on a tin trunk filled with yellowing documents, which lets out a slow sigh and no small amount of dust. There are so many things she doesn't know – about him, about Grace, about him and Grace. But that is what he came here to do: to tell her as much of it as he can bear to speak, and she can bear to hear. What that does to either of them is a thing he can't yet see – and that doesn't matter. All that matters is that he shoves the whole bloody mess of it in her face.

'I was expecting her to come to the house that afternoon,' he says, starting again somewhat randomly – but starting again nonetheless.

'Grace?'

'Of course Grace. Who the fuck else are we talking about?'

She gulps, stares, tries her best: 'And – why was that?'

'Because she wanted to get married.'

'Married?'

He can still hear it: after all this time, she is still thinking of the girl as something separate, whose marriage means almost nothing, whose future husband is not even worth a thought.

'She wanted to ask for a few days off,' he says, as calmly as possible. 'But she never did ask, did she?'

'Well, obviously not. What are you trying to say to me, Looksmart?'

Yes, that was what he understood on that day: that for Patricia, Grace was in another category: like that cry of hers they heard, she was slightly less than human. And this small fact, it was enough to change every other fact between himself and Patricia. It undid every single one of Patricia's acts of kindness, if acts of kindness they ever were. And it was on this small fact that he would build his hate.

'At first I can't believe what I'm seeing,' he says. 'Her head down, not wasting any breath for screaming – and then the dog, the Baas's dog, black and silent, galloping fast – it is three, then two, then one pace behind her.'

There is a terrible silence in the room now: the silence is waiting for him to speak into it. All the world has gathered itself towards this moment of speech, and he has to pick his way across the silence carefully, deliberately, like one stepping across a line of stones that stands over a raging torrent: yes, the silence is roaring at them from its black throat.

'Then Grace is — she is like a double creature,' he continues, 'she is half a woman, half a dog, and she utters a sound so horrible, I don't even recognise it as her, as coming from her — but it brings a dozen farm workers into the garden within seconds. They gather around, like men around some — sacrifice. And they are mute, they are mute with horror. And me — whenever I am trying to approach, the dog is swivelling around, so that Grace, she is always standing between us — always, she is coming between us — and Grace, she is wailing in a strange way, repeating the same few notes again and again, until her voice is finding the right rhythm, the right level, the right song for the pain.'

'Are you all right?' she says.

He wonders what has happened: there's an alien howling in the room, and it takes him a moment to understand that the sound is coming from him.

Patricia

It is not, of course, a scene she is likely to forget — but whenever she has thought about it, she has never recalled Looksmart being there. He is not a part of the picture, not as she recollects it. In her head, he was gone by then, and she was alone, and had to deal with the whole sorry affair herself.

What she can recall is her irritation with the girl. The dog would never have bitten her had she not provoked it — isn't that what Richard said? — and when it finally pulled itself free, instead of remaining where she was and talking the dog down, she turned and ran off screaming — so what else could the dog do but attack?

She also remembers how useless the other workers were, standing around like men turned to stone, waiting as usual for the Madam to step in and help. Why wouldn't Looksmart admit that it was she — Patricia — who stepped in and got the dog off the girl? She grabbed it by the collar and dragged it all the way into the house — half throttling it, the pink foam swaying from its lips, its eyes white and wild, its tongue scarlet with their intermingled blood.

She locked the dog in the guest loo, and when she returned later, there was blood all over the white tiles, as if someone had cut their wrists in there, had second thoughts and tried in vain to get out.

Patricia would have shot that dog if Richard hadn't stopped her.

'She was only doing her job,' he told her. 'You think they'll ever mess with her again after that?'

But they did mess with her after that. One day they found Chloe lying dead at the end of her chain – poisoned, according to the vet. And that, as far as she was concerned, was the last of it.

'What was that girl to you?' she asks him.

She has already understood the answer to this, but she wants him to speak: even his words, which hurt her like a succession of knives, would be better than this, this rootless sobbing wandering about, trying to find a place to settle.

'The man she wanted to marry,' she says. 'It was you, wasn't it?'

Bheki

The rain is so fine it feels like pins and needles on his lips.

Then he sees a man bursting onto the veranda, no more than a silhouette against the window, gulping in the night air as if the whole house is on fire and a dead man's shadow is managing to escape.

Looksmart

He runs outside across the uneven lawn and retches in the rosebushes. There isn't much in his stomach. A cup of tea and a half-eaten biscuit, and the remnants of that lunch in Harrismith. The roses gleam in the darkness, wet with mist, smelling of a childhood that was closed to him. How innocuous they are – growing there with that clarity of purpose that defines plants, blessed with a complete absence of consciousness.

He fumbles in his pockets for his keys and finds only the fruit knife. The keys he left on the mantelpiece, next to the apple. He will have to go back in there to get them, but he will not address another word to her, he will not look at her – he will enter as neutrally as he would his own house, and pick up his keys, and go. He was a fool for coming here. But what did he expect? A miraculous transformation? Nothing has changed. People like her are still sitting in their houses. People like him are still looking in.

'Ukahle nje?'

He knows it's Bheki, the old driver. He can still feel the quiet repressed authority of the man. Even back then Bheki was one of those who spoke only when he had some impressive thing to say. He was also the only worker on the farm who was allowed to touch her car. Standing at the stables, his clothing not far from rags, Looksmart would watch the man driving past. At times Bheki would even be alone in the car, as if the car were actually his and he was off on some noble mission, not on his way to replenish the washing powder.

Later Looksmart understood that it was the car he admired more than the man in the car. By then Looksmart had gained more access to the car himself, and at weekends he was even allowed to wash it. Every mirror and button he polished with a lover's deliberation, every trace of dog he tried to wipe out. Yet cleaning the car reminded him of what he did not have: by the end, the car always gleamed in a way that excluded him.

Before he left the farm forever, Looksmart had learned to despise Bheki. He was little more than a puppet in the front seat, with the Madam in the back seat pulling the strings.

'Ngingasiza?'

Looksmart stands up so the other man can see him, the measure of him.

'Bheki?'

'Ya. Ungubani wena?'

'Phiwayinkosi. But you will know me as Looksmart.'

'Oh, ngiyakhumbula manje. Ubuyile?'

'I have come back. Yes. But not for good.'

He lets the ambiguity of this breathe, suspecting that Bheki will be deaf to it.

'Uzele isidlo sasebusuku?'

'It is more of a – surprise visit.'

Looksmart doesn't know why he is insisting on English. Maybe to mark the change that has occurred between them since they were last together – to make it known to this man who barely used to look at him that he has outgrown him, and outgrown the farm. He knows it is rude of him, yet the older man doesn't seem to be offended.

'I am the one who –'

He wants to tell Bheki what he is here to do, what his job is, but he finds himself stopping short. Power lies with those who withhold their information from others. If you give yourself away, you no longer own yourself. You become the property of others — your secrets passed about from person to person like money, fingered all over by the tacky hands of gossip, until there is almost nothing of you left.

'I wanted to see the old woman one more time before she is gone.'

'Ngiyabona.'

'So you are going with them to Durban tomorrow?'

'Yebo.'

'What about your family? Do you have children?'

'Nginengane eyodwa, uBongani.'

Looksmart doesn't comment on the boy's name: what, after all, do Bheki and his kind have to be thankful for? From inside his jacket, he extracts his cigarettes. He lights one in such a way that Bheki can get a better look at him.

'Would you like a cigarette?'

He knows that Bheki won't refuse a cigarette, in spite of his veneer of dignity. Underneath, he's as needy as the rest of them. He offers the packet before Bheki has answered him.

And for a while they smoke.

'The old Baas,' Looksmart says, with the trace of derision that is used by anyone who has known the farm. 'Have you found him yet?'

'Cha.'

Bheki says this with the same trace of derision, and Looksmart decides that he and Bheki are perhaps not so dissimilar after all.

'She says he has gone mad.'

'He is not so bad — as everyone thinks,' Bheki says in English, this time the ambiguity apparently unintended.

'You mean he's faking it?'

'He will find his way back home to the house tonight. That is his habit.'

They use English with a certain awkwardness, like two people who imagine they are being overheard. Yet their shared knowledge about the old man can be disguised better in English. For them, English remains the language of lies and liars.

There is a long line of bricks and broken cement where the stables used to be. It looks like those shallow graves made during the Anglo-Boer War, where the bodies of the dead were thrown into trenches and covered up before the scavengers could get at them. Had he permitted himself, Looksmart might have found the presence of something ghostly all about him, as though it were his dead lying there under all that rubble – his ancestors, not the old woman's. His ancestors might have wanted to know what he was doing there, what he was hoping to achieve, but he has long ago learned to stamp such thinking out.

Meanwhile, the other man has reverted to isiZulu – carrying on about why he has agreed to go to Durban. It seems there is a problem regarding the man's child. The one his parents wanted to be thankful for. The boy has been marked out as a thing that needs special attention, the kind of attention he hasn't been able to get on the farm.

Looksmart can hear the old woman's voice running through all of this: if you come with me to Durban, I will look after your son. What he has learned to understand and the older man hasn't, however, is that the world runs not on charity, not on kindness, but on money. When you have money on your side, you get to say what must happen and what must not. He gazes at the ruin of the stables in front of him and smiles.

'You don't have to leave this place,' he says.

'Angizwanga?'

'I know the people who are taking over the farm.'

'Ubazi kanjani labantu?'

'I know because I am one of them.'

Bheki stops and peers towards him, trying to make him out.

'Uthini?'

'I'm saying that if you don't want to go down to Durban, you can stay here on the farm. I will give you work. I can help you, and I can help your son.'

Beauty

Yesterday she caught one of uBaas's chickens and turned it into soup. It will be their last meal on the farm. For much of the day the chicken has been bubbling in the pot, along with the remaining potatoes and carrots from the old vegetable patch. There's also a jug of cream from the last cow and a bowl of croutons she made from the bread Bheki got from the village that morning. In the fridge door she finds a lump of glossy cracked cheese, which she grates into the four bowls. Then she fills the bowls to the brim. She knows that Looksmart might be expecting supper, but she has not been asked to provide for him: the soup is watery enough as it is, and she has only made enough for the Wileys, Bheki and herself.

It has been quiet for a while from the sitting room. She hopes he has said what he came here to say and then left. He was always reputed to be a boy with too many words inside his head, thinking himself too clever to listen to the sound of anyone else. In her experience, people don't often change:

the thing you find in them when you first meet them can still be found there afterwards, no matter what words they might use to confuse you. It's like uBaas: almost everything he has ever known has drained out of him, yet she gets the same feeling from seeing him as she got when she first encountered him. He doesn't know his own name half the time, and yet he's still defending himself against the same hurt.

She puts only one bowl on the thin tin tray and anoints it with salt and pepper. She knows exactly how to cater for each one of uMesis's tastes: how she likes her tea, how she likes her toast cut and her oats cooked. She knows how to lay the table, fold the linen, open and close the windows, exactly how and when uMesis desires it. In fact, she knows how to place every single object in the house. In the new house, it will be difficult to begin this process all over again. But uMesis is also too old and too weak to look into cupboards and order things about, so there will be more opportunity for Beauty to arrange things as she likes.

UMesis is sitting exactly as she was before: far back in the chair, with that blasted look across her face. But Looksmart himself is gone.

'Nginesobho lakho, Mesis.'

'Thanks, Beauty. You can put it over here on the trunk.'

'Uphi uLooksmart?'

'I don't know. Is the car still there?'

Beauty goes over to the window and finds the exact picture that was there before: the car is standing under the tree in the rain. Only everything is steeped in darkness, and the silence of the hills is pressing in around the house. The mystery of everything they are is reflected back at her in the black glass, her breath misting up the image of herself.

'It is still there.'

She can't help but sound disappointed by this, but uMesis doesn't ask her about it. She only looks more pained, more pained than usual.

'Did you make Looksmart some chicken soup?'

'Yebo, Mesis.'

'Thank you. You can bring it through.'

'Yebo, Mesis.'

Beauty would like to leave the room, but she can feel a question sitting inside uMesis. UMesis seems to be finding it difficult to approach the question, or otherwise she can't yet find the words to reach for it.

'Did he love her?' she asks at last.

Beauty knows exactly what she is talking about.

'Sorry, Mesis?'

'Looksmart. Was he in love with your sister, Grace?'

'I do not know – anything about that.'

UMesis looks at her – for a moment – as though she wants to see the world through Beauty's eyes. But the look lasts only for an instant, because they both know that such a thing can never be done. Even those who see each other every day are finally blind to one another.

'Looksmart says he was still here. On the farm. When the dog attacked. But I'm sure I would have remembered – a thing like that.'

Beauty can see there is no use denying this. Sometimes a small amount of the truth is enough to satisfy a person's appetite. The challenge is to know which words to end at.

'He was here.'

'You remember that?'

'He was on the farm. He went away after.'

UMesis nods, taking her word for it.

'And were they connected – Grace and the going away?'

'I was still a girl, Mesis. I don't know what was connected or what was not.'

'Perhaps.'

It is possible uMesis suspects she knows more about all this, but there is nothing she can do about it: you can't force a person to speak.

'Can you tell me what you do remember from that day?'

'Not much of a thing, Mesis.'

'Please – you can tell me anything.'

It is true that she could say anything: she could make the words up. But she is not used to using words in the way of Looksmart. She has never had so many words inside her head – even in isiZulu.

'I was there,' she says, 'when they were putting sis' Grace into the car. I remember because Bheki was away from the farm then. He was wanting to get married to a girl from Estcourt – and he went away at that time for some months.'

'Yes, I think I remember that.'

'And for those few months it was Looksmart who was driving your car.'

'Yes – of course. Looksmart had recently got his licence, hadn't he?'

She says nothing to this. She can see uMesis wants to think about anything but the moment of putting the girl in the car. But Looksmart, and the weight of his presence in the room, hauls her back to it.

'And so it was Looksmart – who drove her to the hospital?'

'He was the one to take sis' Grace.'

It feels like they are both looking down a long tunnel – all the way back to that day that neither of them has ever wanted to think about. This is the achievement of Looksmart, even in his absence: to bring them back to that half-forgotten day, which has come to resemble a dream more than an event experienced by each of them.

'Where were you when the dog attacked?'

'I was at the dairy, Mesis.'

'So you didn't see anything.'

This is what uMesis prefers to think, so Beauty lets her think it.

'All you saw was her being loaded into the car.'

Beauty doesn't like the word 'loaded', but she nods anyway.

'And who did it? Who put her into the car?'

'It was Looksmart and the boys from the stables.'

'And then he drove her to the hospital?'

'Yebo, Mesis.'

'Just the two of them?'

'That is what I remember.'

UMesis looks satisfied.

'Thank you, Beauty. We'll – we won't speak about this again.'

'Ngiyabonga, Mesis.'

UMesis leans over her pain – as one would over a low wall – and picks up her bowl of soup. She tastes it to test it and seems to like what she finds there: the temperature as well as the taste. Then she takes a second spoonful to indicate to Beauty that she can go, and that all is well with the soup.

Looksmart

At first he thinks she is a trick of the light: that shape up there on the stoep, hunched up and expectant. Then he sees it is indeed she – the Madam – in a wheelchair. He recalls seeing the wheelchair in the room before, but it still comes as a shock to see her sitting in it so naturally. She must have heaved herself up and wheeled herself out of there. Perhaps she came looking for him, hoping to find him gone. Perhaps she just came to sit on her stoep one last time, her gaze reaching out across the land. It wouldn't have mattered to her that the land was no longer hers: she was born with that gaze, and it would no doubt long outlast any news of her defeat.

'You will catch your death out here, Madam,' he says, relieved to be sounding more like himself.

'Oh, I'm used to this weather. I'm breathing it in. I shall miss it.'

'The bad weather?'

'The mist, the rain. I've never liked the heat. God knows why I ever thought I could be happier in Durban.'

He shakes his head, but she doesn't seem to see him.

'I will never understand,' he says.

'What?'

'Your kind.'

'I have a kind?'

She sounds testy, impatient for him to leave her in peace. From her point of view, this visit is probably not what she might call a success. But he has barely begun.

'Oh ja,' he says, 'sitting up there, waiting to see what'll come down your driveway. Pretending everything's like it should be — when you know that it's not.'

He knows he's probably saying things she's heard before, but what's different this time is that she's hearing it from him — the one who was once the receptacle of all her hope.

He steps onto the stoep and whirls her back into the house. He finds the wheelchair is easier to handle than a child's pram. It lets out a faraway rumble — like a thunderstorm coming in from the hills — as they re-enter the lounge.

At once he sees the two bowls of soup: the one on the trunk that has been emptied into the old woman, and the other still brimming on the mantelpiece, next to his keys. He can imagine what the girl intended by this placement: once he has eaten, the next logical thing for him to do will be to leave the farm, preferably forever.

'I see Togo has brought me some soup.'

When he was a boy, Beauty was sometimes called by her African name: Togo. Beauty he considers a rubbish name, like Grace. Beauty and Grace were popular names in his generation. The poor mothers wanted to raise their daughters up a bit, out of the dirt — like one of those sunflowers that appeared in the compound yard, where the chickens were fed and nothing had ever been asked to grow. The real name of Grace was Noma, like his daughter.

'Do you eat chicken soup?' Patricia is saying. 'It's a bit disgusting, I'm afraid. But I never have the heart to tell Beauty.'

Having manoeuvred her through the maze of boxes and spilled rosettes, he parks the wheelchair next to her chair. While she lowers herself back into her former position, he pushes the wheelchair away and picks up the soup. There is a lump of blanched cheese floating at the heart of it. Without thought, he sits down on a trunk and slops the stringy stuff into his mouth.

'It is indeed disgusting,' he says.

Neither of them smiles, but it's perhaps the first thing that evening they've agreed on.

Patricia

When he is finished – surprising them both with his hunger – he leans back against the wall. She doesn't know what's inside the box he's sitting on, but it doesn't matter now. His knees are higher than looks comfortable and his trousers have been pulled up to expose his socks, which are red and no doubt intended to match the tie. She notices then that the tie has been removed, and that a bit of it is hanging out his jacket pocket, giving the suit a tired look, as though it is panting.

Looksmart

'Beauty told me that you were there,' she tells him. 'She said that it was indeed you who drove her sister to the hospital.'

Patricia says this like it's a huge concession, like she's big enough to admit when she's wrong — even if she's still right in any other way that might matter.

'And what else did she confirm for you?'

He is feeling stronger after the soup. He imagines he can see to the very edge of the farm, all the way to the little barbed wire fence out there in the rain, which would be as easy to pull up as a weed, but is more enduring than anyone who has walked the earth.

'But she seemed to know nothing about you and Grace,' Patricia continues with her usual complacency, 'or your relationship.'

'That is because no one knew,' he says.

'What — not even your mother?'

He is not being entirely honest with her. He never mentioned his ideas of marriage to his mother because he knew she would object. He was too young, and she and her family had no money to pay the lobola. But, most importantly, she had far higher ambitions for her son. What was the point of all that schooling – she would have said – if you're just going to marry a simple-minded farm girl from the dairy?

'No one has ever known about me and Grace,' he says. 'She was killed before we could announce it.'

She nods at him without agreement. She seems to need to rock the words around in her head before they can be slotted into their proper place.

'So you are the only person I've actually told – about Grace.'

'And why is that?'

When he says nothing, she adds: 'I'm afraid I still don't understand any of this.'

'Wait a bit.'

'What about your husband?' he says – when they have waited a bit.

'What about him?'

'Won't he be eating any soup?'

She lifts her head in order to receive his wit more directly.

'He might. There is no end to Beauty's chicken soup.'

There is a moment, once again, when both of them could smile, but neither of them takes it.

'What did you mean earlier? When you said you might have bumped into him?'

'I was only trying to be mysterious.'

'You were trying to frighten me?'

'Did I succeed? Are you frightened yet?'

He can see that no matter how unhinged by him she might become, the last thing she will want to do is show it. Perhaps right now this choice is about all she has left.

'Everything is frightening if you let it be,' she says. 'Waking up in the morning, opening your eyes, contemplating the day ahead. So you can also be frightening if you want to be. Is that what you want to be?'

'I don't know what I want to be.'

He stands and walks over to the large window at the far side of the room. With his back firmly turned against her and all her detritus, he tries again to speak.

'You know what I can't forgive?'

'Sorry?'

'It is that you wanted to protect your seats.'

'My what?'

He knows he has her attention now. Something in his tone has woken her up. They are circling a thing in him that she can't comprehend — that not even he can comprehend. It feels like a wound, descending into him like a deep well, and they are both about to peer right into it.

'Beauty said I put her sister in the car,' he says, ' and that we drove off alone. What else did she say about it?'

'She said Bheki was away at that time, trying to get married, and that you had been driving my car — and then of course it all came back to me.'

'What came back to you?'

'The way you used to love driving my car.'

'That old trash can? Ja, I suppose I did like driving it.'

'It was a good car.'

'Still new, as I recall. Is it the same one that still stands outside?'

'Yes — it's probably the last new car we ever bought.'

He keeps his back to her as he continues, not trusting himself to look at her, keeping his voice level, as though explaining the complex mechanism of a machine to a child.

'I wrap her up in a horse blanket,' he begins, 'and carry her towards your car. But you tell me you don't want her there. You see, you don't want her blood on your seats. You never say this, but I can see you — thinking it.'

'But that's —'

'Instead you say we must go in the bakkie. So I carry her across to the dairy — but when I get to the dairy, there is no bakkie. The Baas has driven it off into the hills. So I come back to tell you, and only then do you say yes — I can take her in your car, the Mercedes Benz.'

'Looksmart —'

'You make us put down blankets, lots of blankets, on the back seat — before I can lay her down, and then I lay her down.'

He swallows the sensation in his throat — a featherless trapped bird clawing to get out — before he can carry on.

'I drive, as fast as I can, to the nearest hospital — was it in Pietermaritzburg? Yes. And. Well — by the time we get there, I think she's fallen into a deep sleep. But she's not asleep, is she?'

When Patricia says nothing, he has to conclude it for her.

'She is dead.'

He remained on the farm long enough for her family to bury her. When he left the next morning, the sun was coming up, and the clouds looked torn to pieces across the sky.

Patricia

The first time she saw Looksmart's mother washing him, she wondered if she should be concerned for him. The mother handled him like he was a piglet, as tough as a piglet, dipping him into the zinc bath and splashing water all over his face. While the infant screamed, almost without pause for breathing, she dried him with a rough grey towel and dressed him.

But it also occurred to her that Looksmart's mother might have been gratified by the sound of his screaming. It would have confirmed for her that the boy was strong: and he would need to be strong in the world he was entering.

On the fifth day after his birth, the umbilical cord fell off. Looksmart's mother said she would bury the piece of flesh – whose flesh exactly? – in the yard where she grew her vegetables.

The baby brought all of them together. Even the dogs would come down to the compound with her every morning after breakfast to see the newborn child. They would walk at her ankles, threatening to trip her up – which they somehow never did – and then lie right against the door of the hut when she went inside. It was impossible to know what the dogs understood about the goings-on inside the hut, but they would whimper and groan, and growl at anyone who approached.

Patricia never tired of watching the baby – the way he lifted his arms and moved his hands slowly and thought about things. Even when he looked full of mischief, he seemed a bit shy somewhere. He would smile without seeming to understand the meaning of a smile. Patricia once said to his mother that he looked like he was receiving signals from faraway ships.

At three weeks, he was able to form proper tears. It was so sad to see him able to cry real tears. It was not long after this that Patricia started to feel the mother's resistance growing towards her. Her visits, which were greeted with a high cry of feigned pleasure, went against the way things were done. So Patricia started to come every second day, then once a week, until it happened that she no longer came at all. She continued to ask about the boy, but he eventually became little more to her than another item on a list – the list of things to be asked about with the workers on the farm.

Once or twice afterwards, the mother carried the child up to the big house at her request. Both mother and child dressed up for these visits, looking like they were on their way to church. The child was brought to her like a foal to be inspected, but he was never offered for her to hold, and Patricia never thought to ask for it.

Looksmart

'But what I have told you is not the full story,' he says. 'It is only about what we saw. What about what we didn't see?'

She is holding onto her hands, as though they are connected to her capacity for speech. He can see that she has submitted herself to this and has finally decided to let him speak.

'When I was carrying Grace towards the dairy, her mouth against my ear, she whispered something so terrible I have never told it to anyone.'

Patricia doesn't move but he can sense that every nerve in her is taut, stretched further with the weight of each word.

'It was your husband,' he says. 'It was your husband Richard who caused it.'

This appears to surprise her. Was she expecting to have to take all the blame for herself?

'How?' is all she can manage.

The words that come between them now are spare, simple, with a great amount of air around them.

'Beauty saw them,' he says.

'Beauty?'

'She walked into that room where the milk tank is. She found them there on the floor.'

'I beg your pardon?'

'Your husband was holding Grace down and he was raping her.'

'Don't be – ridiculous.'

She whispers this word 'ridiculous' as though it's a habit and she means its opposite – as though she is actually wondering what it might feel like to believe him.

'He never saw Beauty,' he says, 'but Grace did. She uttered that shriek we heard, and she shoved him off.'

'I don't believe one word of –'

Again she says this as though she means the opposite: her words are empty, an unhinged tent flapping in the wind with nothing on the ground left to protect.

'But Beauty must have seen another thing,' he continues. 'Remember how your husband used to take that dog Chloe around with him? He would chain it to a fence, a tap, a bush – to stop it from attacking us. Well – on that day, when Grace ran away screaming, he unchained the dog outside the dairy – and he let it loose on Grace.'

'He did what?'

'He unchained the dog and then he climbed into his bakkie – and he drove away into the hills.'

She sits quite still, her hands still clasped to her. There is not a thing moving inside the house: every bit of it, every brick, every cupboard, every pane of glass feels alert.

'You are calling my husband a murderer?'

'That is exactly what I am calling him.'

The same silence: nothing has happened yet, even though everything has happened. The whole house still holding its breath, waiting to see if what has been said might be unsaid – and released into some grand and elaborate joke. But this is not a joke.

'That is not a word to use lightly.'

'And I do not use it lightly,' he says, with all the care he can muster.

Richard

He is plunging through the darkness, crying out for his wife. Earlier he tried to find her name, but when he put his fingers in his mouth all he found there was a wet sock. He has lost all sign of a path. If there were stars to guide him, or a moon, there might be hope, but wherever he goes there's only more rain and sludge and grass, with the occasional rock or porcupine hole to trip him up.

Then he stops at what looks like the house. But this is even less of a house. No more than a floor with what appear to be metal spikes sticking out of it. Here he finds the same bricks rising up, and a black plastic sheet over more bags of cement. Each time, the house less built. Is it that he is going further back in time? Is he going backwards the more he runs? If so then when will he stop? What is he aimed at? He stands on the large concrete slab in the middle of nowhere and ponders this, and eventually he sits.

It is not so much that he is dead. It is more that no one appears to have been born. They still have their whole lives ahead of them. Nothing that needs to be undone has yet been done. Which would be a cause for celebration if he didn't feel so trapped in the mundanity of his surroundings: the concrete slab, darkness all around, the smell of bog. Moreover there is no one else about, no one to share his discovery with. Come to think of it, there isn't anyone to help him with the house. No builders, no uninvited guests, not even the affliction of his wife.

As there isn't much else to do and it's getting too cold to sit, he gets up as fast as his bones will allow and starts to gather together some mud and bricks. It's best to begin any endeavour with modesty, with pragmatism, he thinks. That means a single room, as square as he can make it, unencumbered by any window or door.

Patricia

She doesn't know what role Looksmart expects her to play: the outraged landowner, the devastated wife, his mother? She has tried out all these parts during her life, and many more – the dutiful daughter, the unhappily married spouse, the dextrous lover, the barren woman, the breeder of Welsh ponies, the invalid, the joker, the nurse – and yet none of these has ever managed to reach anyone or change anything. She has watched people do what they would have done anyway, whether she interceded or not. In the end, she was left to fall back on herself, alone in the sitting room, surrounded by dogs that were sleeping their lives away – and were about as effectual as she was.

But he is staring at her nonetheless, full of an expectancy that appears almost optimistic. This is possibly what he came here for: her scepticism. He may have come to doubt his memories and have a scepticism of his own: by refuting her doubts, he will finally be able to banish his.

'Did you at least question Beauty?'

'When?'

'I don't know, Looksmart. Before you left.'

'Who would the police have believed? Your husband or me?'

She doesn't try to answer this — knowing no answer is expected.

'If I'd stayed, I might have killed him. I might have buried my hands deep inside of him — and drawn out his heart.'

He was barely able to look in Richard's direction back then, let alone get anywhere near his heart, but she is not about to say this.

'I'm sorry. But I find all of this difficult to — digest. My husband is far too much of a bigot —'

'To fuck a black girl? Evidently not.'

There was a long line of stable girls from England. She doesn't know exactly how he found them. The back pages of the *Horse and Hound*? In those days, it was easy enough to lure young women mad about horses over from England. They had all been pretty — had he insisted they enclose a photograph? — and posh. And taking a gap year, generally. She liked to think that most of them resisted his advances, but that never stopped him from making them anyway.

It was difficult to believe, but Richard had been a good-looking man once, with his strawberry blond hair, his neat mouth and his pale blue gaze. He had humour and a sly Yorkshire sensuality. Also, he was adept at flattery — and women, in her experience, could rarely resist flattery when it gave the illusion of being accurate. During their brief courtship, he had managed to divine much of what she had always wanted to hear. The narrative she had told herself and had never had repeated back at her. She was her own person, good at kissing, wise beyond her years. He even claimed to like her bouncy hair and oversized breasts. On occasion he would suckle her like a baby while she stroked his hair.

The first girl from England had upset her, she didn't mind admitting that. But in the end it was what permitted her affair a few years later with John Ford. She was pleased — on the rare occasions she thought about it now — that her relationship with John endured long after the last of the stable girls had left. She liked to think she had outlasted Richard in this, as in everything else.

And she had found more than enough opportunity to punish Richard for his antics. First she denied him her body, then her bedroom, then her friendship, and finally she denied him her imagination. It was this last retraction that might have been her mistake, for what other acts had he committed during her absence?

'Even if it's true —' she hears herself saying, 'even if he did have sex with her. God knows, he might have, he tried to seduce a long line of stable girls from England. Even then, you can't say he set the dog on her. That is just — a monstrous thing to say. Especially when you don't know the facts.'

'And what facts are those?'

'Don't you know that she was taunting the dog, throwing stones at it, and that it pulled itself free?'

She's embellishing, of course — not so much to defend herself as to test him, or break his momentum.

'Who told you that?'

'Well — Richard did.'

Looksmart laughs and shakes his head — but what does it matter, whether he believes her now or not? Who's to say what happened on that barely discernible day? Not her, and certainly not Looksmart.

'And I'm sorry,' she continues, 'but there was nothing — nothing at all about going to the dairy to get the bakkie. We loaded her straight into the Merc and you drove it away at once.'

'Just now you couldn't even say I was there, but now you can tell me that? Come now, Madam. Surely you can do better than this!'

'As we are speaking, it's all — it is all coming back.'

It is true: the more she speaks her version of events, the clearer they become, each detail fitting neatly into place. For what's to make his account any more accurate than hers? She knows that he is doing exactly what she is doing: making up sentences as he goes along, bridging whatever gaps he encounters as he encounters them.

'Then you will know that it was me who carried her to the dairy and all the way back again, while you — you hid in the house.'

'I was securing the dog, or trying to find Richard. Does it matter what? All I know is – I would never have cared about getting blood on my seats!'

As she says this, she believes it, she has never believed anything as firmly as she believes it.

'You're going to deny even that?'

'But by your own admission, I never even said it!'

'You thought it!'

He reels away from her as though everything around him is about to implode.

'You said we had to take her to the bakkie, and when she had to go in your car you made us to put down blankets – flea-bitten blankets you reserve for your dogs. Of course you thought it, man!'

There has always been fighting in this house. Objects thrown about, shouting, recriminations going deep into the night. And although she and Richard haven't fought for some years – mainly because he's become incapable of sustaining a satisfying argument – his rage has not diminished. And neither has hers. There are times when they still shout in each other's direction without any apparent provocation. By raising their voices against the vacancy, they are reminding themselves that they exist and can still feel something.

So Patricia is used to shouting. Were they speaking of something else, she might even be partially enjoying this: this exchange with Looksmart reminds her of a world in which things matter, where people still want to be heard, and where there are consequences to their actions.

'Listen, Looksmart. I really don't know what happened. Or why it has to matter now. Why you're wasting time on this, on me, on things that are dead. You have a wife, children – a splendid bloody suit!'

'It's because I want you to understand!'

'What?'

'What I understand!'

Beauty

She is running along the road, the same road Grace ran along all those years ago, but she is running in the opposite direction, towards the rubble where the dairy once stood. The rain is falling, slow and heavy as salt, all through the farm and all through the valley – and all the way up to the crooked peaks of the Drakensberg. Everything is lost in this rain, everything is lost. She has been calling for Bheki and calling uBaas, and it feels like she is alone on the farm, maybe the last person left. Of course, there are those two people in the sitting room, in the only place where there is any light, but they are like ghosts, taken away by the past, but still blind to one another and unaware of the night that has grown up all around them.

'Bheki!'

The only person she wants is Bheki. She wants to hold onto his overalls and weep into him. She wants his tallness and stillness and his long arms around her. She wants to breathe in the smell of him – like a hayfield in the heat of summer – and lean into the peace of him until the storm has passed.

'Bheki!'

But there is no sign of Bheki. There is only the rain and the mud. She has been running along the same track since she was a girl, always in the opposite direction from Grace, never straying from the path, and now there is nothing left ahead of her but a heap of broken bricks.

Looksmart

'The first thing I saw on getting back from boarding school,' he says, 'was a black puppy, playing in the garden, chewing a rubber ball to bits. The second was Grace, the most beautiful thing I had ever seen. As our love grew, that dog in the garden was growing too. My love and your fear, they grew together. And now, I can no longer separate them. When I think of one, I see the other. I see that double thing, that creature – the beast. Circling the garden, dripping blood.'

'What can I say to that? Do you expect me to make it any better?'

'But you gave up. You withdrew exactly when it was your moment to step forward and – do something, change something. Save her! I thought you cared, but you didn't. I thought I meant something, but I didn't. All you cared about was protecting your seats!'

The words are happening elsewhere. He is far away from them. Instead he is standing in the garden, hardly bigger than a boy, watching the beast. He has never really left this place. Well, for a while he did everything he could to leave this place, but it was always there to meet him – there where he least expected it. Then his marriage happened and his children, and he tried to lead each member of his family back to that garden to salvage the boy who was stuck there. His wife failed first. Initially she suspected something was missing in her husband, an organ that could have pulled the rest of him into a more coherent whole. But eventually she gave up and these days, he often thinks, she has probably come to believe there was never any organ missing after all. His daughters, however, are still looking for that missing part of him. Because they feel complete, they expect him to be. They haven't yet reached the first moment of their disappointment – when they find in him a vacancy to meet the abundance that is in their hearts.

There are tears leaking from his face, but this is happening far away and is not his business, and meanwhile the words are carrying on.

'I don't know what you're saying,' she is saying, 'but yes, maybe I did do something, maybe I was thinking about my seats when I should have been thinking about her. Maybe I got it wrong and wasn't being – whatever it was you wanted me to be. And you're right: I was probably bloody resentful that I had to have all of that happening there, on my front lawn, without any of us being able to do a thing about it. I simply can't remember. Can't you believe that? Can't you accept that all of this – it's lost?'

'Lost? It isn't lost,' he tells her. 'I think about it every day.'

Patricia

Beauty arrives covered in mud. Usually she would have removed her shoes at the kitchen door, wiped away the muck with a cloth and gone barefoot or changed her shoes, but this time she seems to have forgotten.

'Mesis, I have looked everywhere and I can't find uBaas.'

Otherwise the mud is intended as a statement: this is the state I am in, or we are in. This is what we have been reduced to.

'Beauty, I wanted to ask you.'

'Mesis?'

'I wanted to ask you more about your sister. Grace.'

'Yebo, Mesis?'

'I would like you to tell me more about the day she died. What you saw at the dairy. And this time I would like the truth.'

The word 'truth' seems to surprise Beauty. Perhaps such a thing has never been asked of her before. Patricia watches her adjusting herself to the word, to the unusual flavour of it. She seems to be preparing herself for it, squaring up to it, like one of those gymnasts you see on the television, about to twist themselves improbably through space.

'Yebo, Mesis.'

'You have nothing to be afraid of.'

'Yebo, Mesis.'

She says this as though Patricia has no idea of what she's talking about.

'There is what you know, Mesis. The dog — that it killed her.'

'Yes, but what don't I know?'

Beauty switches her gaze away from the vistas such a question might open up and instead feigns a general impotence.

'Mesis?'

'Before the attack,' Patricia says, 'at the dairy. What exactly did you see?'

A scene seems to flicker before her eyes. Back and forth, back and forth — and back again. But Beauty does not appear to like what she sees. Or perhaps she does not like what it might lead to. She looks frightened in a way Patricia has never seen in her before.

'Lutho, Mesis.'

'Then why do you look so afraid?'

Looksmart approaches her without a sound. With a new voice, he speaks, full of what sounds like feigned compassion.

'Ungesabi, Beauty. Siyalazi iqiniso.'

She has a quick flash at him, something like annoyance, suggesting that nothing he can say will make any difference, either way. He is not the thing to be afraid of: the thing to be afraid of — that she carries inside her.

'You do not know the truth,' she tells him.

'Beauty, you must not be afraid.'

'Mesis — but I can't say it.'

Even Patricia can see that this is her way of telling them that she might be able to say it, but only with the right prompting.

'My husband is a sick man now,' Patricia says. 'If you're the only one who saw the whole of what happened and can still remember — well, then, you have to speak.'

Beauty is looking at a thing ahead of her from different angles, perhaps wondering if there is any way to circumvent it. But she can't get around it: it is coming towards them ineluctably, like a sneeze or a death.

'I will not blame you,' Patricia adds. 'I can promise you that.'

When the words finally come, they come from a resigned and inevitable place. The story she is about to tell sounds familiar to her, as if she's played it a thousand times inside her head. But even as she hears the words, Patricia knows they are only making a gesture in one general direction: a row of miniature arrows, no more effectual than chopsticks, making a stab at a city's walls.

'I was finishing with the cows, letting them out into the – I was about to do the cleaning with the hosepipe, and, and, and –'

'And?'

'I was turning the tap when – the noise, it is coming from the storage room, so I open the door a little bit, very soft, so I can see – and then I see.'

'What do you see, Beauty?'

Looksmart asks this, trying to hold her there with his voice, almost caressing her, like a hypnotist. But she is far away, wrapped deep inside herself, hardly daring to breathe.

'They are on the floor, aren't they?' Looksmart says.

'Yes.'

'His hand is over her mouth.'

'She sees me, and –'

'Qhubeka, Beauty!'

But for a moment she can't seem to carry on.

'Did she get away from him then?' Patricia says.

'Yebo, Mesis.'

'And the dog,' Patricia continues, 'did my husband unchain the dog?'

'Oh, Mesis!'

Beauty starts to breathe more rapidly, panting like a dog – like the dog they are talking about. But it reminds Patricia more of a woman trying to give birth.

'Tell us, Beauty!'

'He undo the chain – and the dog running.'

Looksmart is standing now, looking over their heads, seeing the scene as he imagines it – expectant, entranced, almost triumphant.

'Yes!' he says. 'He waits to see the dog catch her, doesn't he? He waits to make sure. Isn't that it, Beauty?'

Beauty doesn't look at him. She barely hesitates. But the scene – or so it seems to Patricia – has already started to fade away inside her, like the light in the eye of a dying animal.

'That,' she says, 'is it.'

Looksmart moves away, shrugging his shoulders as if wanting to remove his jacket. It is a gesture of relief, of release. Perhaps he now imagines he will be free from his burden. But he will never be free. All he has achieved is to hand some of his burden across to Patricia.

'When the police came to question everyone – why did you say nothing?' Patricia says.

'I was young. No one ever looked at me. And I was – I was afraid of him.'

'Yes, I see,' Patricia says, seeing it all with a strange and estranging clarity. 'And Richard – does he even know what you saw?'

'No one knows what I saw.'

Beauty seems to say this with the knowledge that this statement, for the first time, is no longer true: two others now know what she saw. What she saw no longer belongs to her: it will become a part of the general story that is used to define her sister.

'Will you say this to uBaas, Mesis?'

Patricia can see that even today the poor woman is afraid of him.

'Tell me, Beauty,' she says, 'did he ever try anything with you?'

'Cha, Mesis.' Beauty throws this idea away with a quiet ferocity. 'Grace – she was the last one from the farm.'

The two women almost seem to have forgotten about Looksmart. Patricia gazes at the small proud spirit in front of her, wondering at the enigma of her. She had come to think of Beauty as her friend and she thought she knew everything there was to know about her – but, of course, that was only vanity, or laziness, or wishful thinking.

'Don't worry, Beauty,' she says – feeling as she says it that she has said it before, and will no doubt say it again, 'we are finished talking about this now.'

'Ngiyabonga, Mesis.'

But still Beauty looks sceptical.

'And what about uBaas?'

'What about him?'

'Do you still want him?'

Four

Beauty

'Kwenzenjani? Ubukeka engathi uqeda ukubona isipoki.'

Bheki is sitting at the kitchen table, his hands in front of him like he's waiting to eat. But there is nothing on the table to eat, only the Toby jug with the beaded net over the top of it to keep away the flies. In all her time on the farm, she has never seen Bheki sitting here, as if he owns the place. And without thinking too much about it, she sits down opposite him, watching his hands, longing to take hold of them. They both remain there for a while, as if waiting for the food to come, while the rain tinkles on the roof and gurgles down the gutters.

'I am the ghost,' she wants to say back to him, 'I do not exist.'

But she says nothing like that. Instead she asks him about uBaas.

'Abakhi bambonile eza nganeno,' he says. 'Bengicabanga ukuthi usebuyile.'

'Akakabuyi,' she confirms: he hasn't come back.

She wonders then if Looksmart might have murdered him. It might have been the first thing he did when he arrived on the farm: to take a long knife and plunge it deep into his heart. And in spite of herself she feels a dark ripple running through her that feels like hope: hope not for his life but for his death, his suffering. Before she knows what she is doing, she takes hold of Bheki's hand. She is breathing with difficulty, but maybe it's only because she's still recovering from the running in the rain.

'Kazi kwenzakalani le?' he says to her. 'Konakelephi?'

But the last thing she can tell him is what is wrong, what is happening. It is not because she has never spoken to him about Grace, or the death of Grace. It is because she doesn't know herself. Now that she has started to speak, she no longer trusts herself to speak: she is afraid of too much truth spilling out.

'Uke wakhuluma noLooksmart?' she asks him instead.

He tells her yes: he has spoken to Looksmart. He spoke to him earlier when he came outside for a cigarette.

'Nikhulume ngani?' she says.

But Bheki withdraws his hand, declining to tell her what he and Looksmart discussed.

When the hand is taken away from her, she stands, trying to swallow the complicated sensation passing through her. Bheki remains sitting there, pretending nothing has happened – even though everything has happened. She knows now that there has been a switch inside him: he has passed over from where she is standing to where Looksmart is standing. He has withdrawn a vital part of himself from her.

Muttering a few words about how she must find uBaas, she opens the door and is about to step back into the darkness and the wetness when she sees something standing there. She thinks at first it's a statue made of mud, then she sees it's a child, covered in muck, shrunken away from the cold – but when it moves she sees that it's uBaas himself, waiting in the rain, forgetting that for a door to open all you need to do is turn the handle or knock.

'Baas? You have come back.'

Bheki comes and stands behind her. For a moment, this feels like their house and uBaas feels like the visitor, the intruder.

'Aren't you going to let him in?'

Bheki asks this with touch of irony: the idea of not letting him in seems to amuse him, amuse him with its impossibility. But instead of opening the flyscreen for uBaas to step back into the house, she steps outside and leaves the flyscreen to slam back shut in Bheki's face.

'Where are you going?' he asks through the wire mesh, still with that new defiant amusement in his voice.

But she doesn't answer him: she is already leading uBaas back into the rain, back along the track she has recently run down, towards the rubble of the dairy and the dryness of her small room beyond it.

'Mama?' uBaas says.

She doesn't respond to this either, but continues down the churned-up track. He is slightly behind her and she is pulling his left sleeve forwards – tugging it, as one would lead a reluctant horse. Everything is slimy with the wetness and mud and she wonders briefly when last she saw the sun.

They enter the dark unfinished house and she takes him through to her room. Because it is in the same position as his room in the original house, she hopes this will serve to comfort him. While he perches on the edge of her bed, she switches on an oil lamp and finds a clean towel from her suitcase – which still sits with misplaced confidence on the bed.

UBaas is spreading a wet mud patch into her sheets, a shiver passing through him. She takes off what is left of his shirt – which is shredded around the wrists and covered in something powdery and grey, maybe cement – and dries him carefully with her towel. There are scratches all over his body, especially his face, and his hands are scuffed and bleeding.

She finds a pale yellow ANC T-shirt from her suitcase and dresses him in this, along with the pink anorak. The lower half of him she decides she will do nothing about, but she removes his shoes and socks and puts her sheepskin slippers on his feet.

'Is this our house?' he says.

'Yebo, Baas.'

'I want us to go home.'

She tells him that he is at home, this is his house — and he gazes around the dim room, noting the boarded-up windows, the rickety nature of the furniture, the beer crate in the corner. She can see that he doesn't believe what she's saying, but that he's sufficiently content: so far, there's nothing in the room he can find to object to.

Patricia

He arrived off a ship from Southampton and came for dinner in Durban: the new manager, fresh out of Cirencester, brought over by her father to run the farm. She can still recall the look of him across the dinner table. His pinkish pale hair and calculating pointed face reminded her of a fox, a fox that had its eye on her potential for eggs. He also spoke as a fox might speak, with an air of tact, sex and cunning.

He was nothing if not polite back then. But his gaze drifted around the room, taking in the polished silver, the paintings of hunting scenes and ships at sea — and the rich man's daughter sitting across from him, with her wayward dark hair and violet-blue gaze. He was awkward with the servants, the furniture, the cutlery, but she saw beneath this a residue of mischief that he occasionally shared with her when no one was looking.

Even then Patricia was a fleshy girl. Buxom, he would later call her. Even then she was far more substantial than he — at least in any way that might have mattered. But he had also come a long way to arrive at that table. Out of the farm where he had been little more than a labourer's son, into a bursary at Cirencester, and across the sea to Durban, South Africa. She liked him for his boldness of vision: little did she suspect that he had used all of it up.

One weekend she drove up to the farm to have another look at him. They went off on his motorbike, to a waterfall, for a swim. The water was so cold it took their breath away. It also made their grey underwear completely transparent – which Patricia chose to laugh at, and he followed suit. Afterwards, they sat on the rocks to dry off, their bodies angled away from each other out of modesty. The sound of the water made it difficult to speak, difficult to think, but a quiet hum started up that both of them carried over the next few weeks.

'I think I owe you an apology,' she says.

'You "think"?'

Since Beauty confirmed his story and left the room, Looksmart's moment of triumph seems to have filtered out of him. He is looking smaller, closer to his true age, full of an uncertainty that she has often recognised in herself.

'But it still seems too easy,' he says.

'What?'

'All of this.'

'None of this is easy.'

Immediately she can see that he has no interest in her demonstrations of regret. Perhaps she doubts they could ever match his.

'But I can't change what happened, Looksmart. Can't you see that? What Richard has done – he has done. And me – well, I will never be able to take back the thoughts I had – that you say I had – when that poor girl lay bleeding.'

He gazes at her, looking worried.

'But – you are sorry?'

She sees he is afraid she'll retract her small apology – not even give him that.

'Of course I'm sorry. How many times would you like me to say it?'

Not to be put off, he carries on looking at her, wondering at her.

'Your apology is all I'm interested in hearing from you,' he says at last. 'Nothing else. For the rest of your days, I want you to be sorry, I want you to be sorry – and I want you to carry on telling me only that.'

For a moment, she suspects him of exaggeration, or at least of trying to make a joke.

'What are you saying, Looksmart? That you want to see me again after this?'

She intends this as a kind of counter-joke, idle and ironic, but he appears to take it literally, as if there really is a part of him that might want to see her again.

'I have no idea – what can happen after this.'

After what? she wonders – for she has hardly any idea of what has passed between them. She knows what he's said, what he's claimed as the truth – but what did he come here for? To shout at her? To cut her husband's throat? Surely for more than a word or two of apology.

'Tomorrow I will be going down to Durban,' she says. 'With Richard – and Beauty and Bheki. What will happen then? Must everything just carry on as it was before?'

'Is that what you want?'

'It doesn't matter what I want. What do you want?'

Beyond his desire to tell her his story – perhaps even to hurt her with his story – he doesn't seem to have given this much thought.

'I suppose what I'm trying to say,' she continues, 'is will you be able to go away from here and try to become something – something new?'

'What are you talking about?'

'I imagine I'm talking about hope.'

'Hope?' he laughs this away with a hint of his old hardness. For him, it seems, hope is a flag waved in a country that has yet to exist. 'Ag – I've tested that one out. And now what do you see? The very picture of success! A man with a car, a wife, two children. Everything I have ever done, I've done it with hope.'

'But that doesn't sound so bad, does it? A wife. Two children. That's a good enough start.'

He shakes his head and murmurs something unintelligible.

'In some ways, you're actually quite fortunate,' she continues. 'You see, I never even managed to have a child.'

But she can see he is not about to relent.

'There's more to a man than a suit.'

'What are you saying? That you are not gratified by your success?'

He moves away so violently that it makes her start – knocking over a box as he goes, and spilling a packet of tiny shiny cabbage seeds across the floor.

'You want me to be grateful?' he says. 'Is that what you want?'

It feels like she's with Richard again, having the same argument: the rug always being yanked out from under her feet as soon as she steps onto it.

'Is that all you've ever wanted? For me to be grateful for all my gifts?'

'You have had opportunities that many would kill for,' she says, hearing in her voice the same tone she uses with Richard. She doesn't quite believe in this tone – she never has – but she has still found it to be effective.

'I have worked hard for every single thing I've got,' he is saying. 'You think it came to me on a plate?'

'I still don't understand what it is you came here for – what it is you want!'

He is pacing again, up and down, back and forth, once more saved by his anger – apparently relieved to have regained it: 'I will tell you what I want for you, old woman. I want for you guilt, darkness! I don't want you to leave this place tomorrow without a backwards glance – and to spend your last days looking, looking at the sea, with your mind all clear, your sleep easy – what I want is for you to remember that dog like I remember that dog, and I want you to be haunted and – and decayed away by it!'

He sits down at the far end of the room with a thump on a trunk too full of papers. His back is towards her, his head pressed again into his hands as if he wants to compress all his thoughts to an entity the size of a walnut.

'I think I understand what you feel,' she says, so softly that he may not hear.

'You do?'

'I also know what it is. To die quietly.'

'I only married him because I was pregnant.'

'Don't you understand? I'm not interested in hearing about any of your rubbish!'

'My father wanted to kill him when he found out,' she says – not really caring whether he is listening or not, 'but I talked to him and he gave us this farm instead. He was a good man, my father. I like to say he was the one good man in my life – and when he died, he died thinking I was happy, hoping I was happy, taking my word for it.'

When he says nothing, she leans towards him and adds: 'But it was only much later, when you started to hang around the house, that I was – that I was happy again for a bit.'

He stares at her out of his grief, looking about as lost as he has ever been. Not knowing where else to plant her gaze, she can only look back at him.

'But – you told me that you never managed to have a child,' he says.

'What?'

'Now you tell me he made you pregnant.'

'I had one,' she says – suddenly not trusting herself to speak.

'And this one child. It is still alive or what?'

'I think that is my business.'

Looksmart

Before he knows what he's doing, he has picked up the trunk he was sitting on and thrown it across the room, towards the mantelpiece. It hits another box and there's an explosion of papers. They flutter downwards, like confetti without a bride under it.

'Well, I want to make it my business!'

He has turned to her, his face snarled against her face: he doesn't know what he's saying, who he is, what is speaking for him, but he knows that now he can't stop it.

'I want to know about this child because once, a long time ago, I thought you cared about another child. You sent me to that school, gave me that blazer, corrected my English – you woke something up and then you killed it – you killed it as surely as you made me to kill that fish!'

'We let that fish go.'

'We didn't.'

'We did!'

'We didn't!'

He reels away and would have walked off into the hills were it not for the walls of the room containing them, making them turn back to each other. It doesn't matter that there's an open door, or that either of them could stop: there's no avoiding this now. It is like thunder rolling through the clouds, its progress marked by a beating of drums that seems to come from under the house itself.

'I gave you everything,' she is saying back at him, gasping for more air. 'Everything you ever asked for. You wanted to go to boarding school, so I sent you, didn't I? Have you forgotten the trunk full of tuck? The labels me and your mother sewed on? The letters — what about the letters I used to write? Every Sunday evening, for five years, I wrote back!'

'And every holiday I came home to sleep in my mud hut!'

They are both breathless with the glory, the sheer relief, of being able to shout: it doesn't matter what words they choose, or that their words might sound ridiculous.

'I gave you work! I taught you all about my roses — and all the different plants. You were hungry to learn. You wanted to know about everything. The names of birds and butterflies, the sicknesses of the horses, the chickens — the way to bake a loaf of bread. Don't you remember that? You were there, every morning as I got up, hanging about, always wanting to help.'

'You gave me work? To cut your lawn and drive your car? You call that work? Maybe it would have been better if you'd left me, there where you found me — in that fucking hut!'

They are finally freeing themselves from the small patch that has stood between them: worn like a prison yard, tramped forever by the same circle of feet.

'It was for pocket money. It's quite normal for children to earn a bit of pocket money, you know. And you loved my car — didn't you always tell me how much you loved it?'

'Tell me about your son.'

'What?'

'What happened to your son?'

She gasps again — aghast — looking for a moment like she might laugh.

'Who said anything about a son?'
'What?'
'It was a girl who died, not a son.'
'And?'
'She was born.'
'And?'
'There were complications.'
'And?'
'She was born dead.'

Patricia

She arrived two months early and two days dead. Patricia awoke in the hospital room to find a hollow wind running through her body where her child had been. They brought the bundle for her to look at. The baby had been cleaned and wrapped in a cloth, but there was no mistaking that she was dead. The tiny grey form, the dark shock of hair, the pale blue eyelids firmly shut against the world – the eyes that would never see, the mouth that would never speak. All those cells dividing and re-dividing, to form a child that lacked nothing except a life – that secret current that comes from nowhere, entering into some forms and forsaking others, randomly – or so it seemed to Patricia.

She looked like she was made from wax, the blood drawn out of her. She was the colour of a bruise, but still she glowed – a quiet yellow light that came from deep inside of her, a moon fading back into her heart. The small head lolled back in a final gesture of abandonment as Patricia took the child in her arms. The body forever lost in the world, without any defence.

Rachel would be forever dead.

The nurses brought her back later in a box the size for shoes. Patricia carried her out the hospital and into another day, the light around her seeming to fall on foreign ground. Richard might have been standing beside her – she didn't remember. And it would be only later that she was able to cry. There would be whole afternoons ahead of her in which there was nothing left to do but weep. The weeping would usually come without warning, sometimes in the car, outside the shops, or on the dirt road leading away from the house. Otherwise it would come while sipping soup, or removing a shoe, or doing nothing at all.

The emptiness in her body, just below her heart, has never left her. She can summon it up merely by thinking about it. A sensation like butterflies trying to get out.

Afterwards, she would not be able to have another child, and with her womb went all her hope. That word she used with Looksmart: hope. Using it as though it had any meaning for her. But perhaps he would have better luck with it than she ever did.

In the days that followed Rachel's death, all she saw was the thin path lying ahead of her, with Rachel's death at the beginning of it and her own death at the end of it. There could be nothing else between. Only her days under the bloodwoods, which sounded like a dark sea, hissing and sighing and swaying around her – always approaching, but never managing to reach her.

'You wouldn't know – what it is to lose a child. It was a time of darkness. Long nights and long days, everything made dark.'

'What about your husband?'

'What about him?'

'Well, how did he deal with it?'

Richard stood around a lot, not meeting her eyes whenever she turned to him. She watched him as he crept away, a lame dog. He tried to hide himself in the farm. Coward. A coward he was.

'Not very well,' she says.

'And you?'

She sat in this chair and kept her mouth shut. She bred Welsh ponies for other people's children.

'I tended my roses.'

'I see.'

She can sense a change in him now. He looks like he's given up on her – or given up on this particular fight. Perhaps he's not so sure what the differences between them are any more. Perhaps the deaths of Rachel and Grace have levelled the land between them and established clearer perspectives.

It is because of this thought that she can say the next thing, which would have been impossible only a few minutes earlier.

'Didn't you know?' she says.

'What?'

'Didn't you know that you are the only child ever to be happy in this house?'

She watches him twist away from this idea. It is a gesture she knows well – and it is a sign of pleasure, not of pain or humiliation. When he was a boy, he would squirm under the knowledge of her gaze exactly like this: on the athletics field and during chapel – and on Speech Day, when there was a snicker every year when he walked away once again with the Zulu prize.

'You were like the sun,' she says. 'My son.'

Carrot cake was his favourite. She would often have one made to welcome him home for the holidays. They would sit on the stoep and he would still be wearing his greys, his military tan shoes and black and white striped tie – always tied in a Windsor knot, as taught by John Ford during Monday morning assembly – and they would munch on the cake while he told her what had happened to him at school since they'd last met. Only when he was finished would she tell him about the farm, which generally involved a list of births and deaths, and the usual glossing over financial loss. She never wondered what he might be glossing over, or when the glossing over might have started.

'And then you started to judge me,' she says.

'I did?'

'I can still see you – standing in the corridor.'

'Doing what, exactly?'

'Looking at all the photographs. With a look of terrible contempt.'

'There was a picture of your husband I used to stare at,' he tells her. 'With the two dead leopards. It used to fascinate me, that picture. I don't know why. But in his eyes there was this expression – like he didn't know what it was he'd lost.'

He glances at the place where the couch was, but there is only a pile of boxes there.

'Where are those leopard skins now?' he says.

'Oh packed away, I expect.'

It wasn't just the photographs he started to judge, it was every object in the house: the crockery, the linen, the size of the taps. Everything around him would come to stand between them – like a wall.

'I thought it was adolescence,' she continues. 'I thought it would pass.'

'What?' he asks, feigning ignorance.

'But it never did.'

This time he doesn't dodge away. He seems to choose to look at her directly, perhaps the better to disguise himself.

'No,' he says, 'it never did.'

It happened so quickly, the loss of Looksmart. She raised the subject with

John Ford once – John apparently being the authority on boys – and was told that boys were like that: one minute they were there, munching on cake, chattering about their day, and the next they'd vanished, leaving dirty socks on the bedroom floor, half-finished mugs of tea in the lounge and the front door agape. John told her to be patient. Even though the boy was not her son, he would be sure to come back. His years with her had been far too significant.

'I wonder if I connected your disappearance and Grace. You know, at the time I might have – I honestly can't tell you now.'

He looks at her as if to suggest that it doesn't matter – or perhaps to suggest that what he thought mattered is not what matters after all.

'But after a while I came to think of you as another dead child.'

He shakes his head, apparently wanting to distance himself from that other child.

'I didn't want to think of you as taking from me and giving nothing back,' she continues. 'You see, it went against my idea of you.'

Looksmart

Looksmart's first school was a small whitewashed building that stood alone under a bluegum tree. In summer the Christmas beetles would emit a constant shrill and the tin roof would groan in the afternoon heat. In winter the room was like a fridge. Not only did it have walls one brick thick, but the windows hadn't been fitted properly and there was a significant gap under the plywood door. But Looksmart barely noticed any of this: from his first day at school, he was in heaven. Soon he was being promoted to the class above him, and the class above that. Until one day his teacher summoned Looksmart's mother and told her the boy had a gift and should apply to a school that was better equipped. Looksmart's mother hadn't forgotten Patricia's earlier attachment to her son, so she went to her to discuss the boy's future – and, without hesitation, Patricia agreed to intervene.

Looksmart was one of the few people who knew about the relationship between Patricia and John Ford. From the moment they met, he observed the way they looked at each other and forgot about him, and how they recalled him only when they had to remind themselves why they were there.

He might have expected to get special treatment because of his inside knowledge, but instead the headmaster never seemed to lose an opportunity to 'put him in his place' – as he called it. Once when it was his birthday, Looksmart was sitting in the dining hall, about to have a cake brought out for him, when he felt a blow that blasted him with stars and sent him clattering across the floor: he had been caught rocking on his chair.

The whole room was silent when he sat up – and John Ford was still standing over him, his hand raised, prepared for another strike.

'You bloody idiot,' was all the teacher said.

The cake – carried by the school chef, Petrus – came bursting through the double doors from the kitchen at that moment, and everyone laughed. It was a complicated laughter that Looksmart – later in life – tried to understand. The contrast between the triumphant cake and the fallen boy was no doubt a part of it. But whatever its meaning, what was clear even then was that the whole school was on the side of the headmaster.

Later, Looksmart went to the toilet area of the hostel to cry. He wanted very badly to cry, but when he sat on the toilet in that cold echoing room, no tears came: instead he felt the first stirrings of what he would later come to know as his hate.

In Looksmart's final year, he was voted in by the staff as a prefect. He and the other prefects would go to the headmaster's house during prep once a month for prefects' meetings, where they ate more cake, this time made by John Ford's dying wife – who had already lost all her hair by then and wore a pink knitted cap she'd made herself. Looksmart remembered one occasion late in the year when he and John Ford drifted outside and urinated together on the grass. The headmaster had said, 'Do you want to kill a mole?' – and Looksmart followed him out into the darkness, not knowing quite what the old man was talking about. As they started pissing companionably, Looksmart could almost imagine liking John Ford, but there had been too many daily acts of brutality to shift Looksmart's attitude in the end. Most of all he disapproved of the way John Ford stood up there in chapel, handing out the bread and wine as if he was closer to God than the rest of them.

Over the years he has encountered several of the boys from his old school. He even worked with one for a while: a rather asinine boy who had never said a word to him when they were at school together, but who greeted him on his first day at work like they were the oldest of friends. Times had certainly changed. But Looksmart was actually grateful for the deception: it gave him a dignity that stretched back.

Since Beauty left the room and the old woman started talking about herself, he has been wishing simply that he could stumble off to one of the rooms and go to sleep for a few hours. He has never slept in this house. He used to imagine what it might be like, slipping into one of those giant beds with their huge sighing pillows. This house seemed to him the very picture of luxury. Only now does he see it for what it was: as a place with no more life left in it.

It has been like using an obscure muscle, this attempt to talk from a place he has never spoken from before. Yet the old woman sounds as perky as ever, as if they have only now started speaking – and all that shouting earlier concerned someone else.

'You know what I would have said if you'd told me you wanted to marry Grace?' she is saying.

'What?'

'I would have told you that you could do better, that you must never marry below yourself – because that's exactly what I did, you see, when I married Richard.'

It's strange to hear her talk of herself and the old man as if they were once young: for him, they have only ever existed as he has liked to imagine them, with their bodies already broken and their lives exhausted.

'If you don't mind, I'd rather not talk about him,' he says.

'Oh, I know that.'

But it's clear as she says this that she hasn't taken offence: she seems to have no desire to talk about her husband either. In fact, she never did. In everything she has ever said or done regarding him, she has always seemed to regard him as already lost.

'What about your wife?'

'What about her?'

'Well, what's she like?'

'She's like you say your father was,' he says. 'She's a good woman – good.'

But then he turns his head away from the light so that she can't see his face. He can't talk about Annabel. Not now, not to the old woman. The old woman is too clever by half and will soon discover the truth.

'And you have been happy?' she continues.

'Sometimes.'

He married Annabel knowing that he didn't love her, but hoping that one day he would. And since then there have been times when he has been sufficiently in love with the idea of her – or the idea of himself with her – that he has believed himself to be content. There have also been moments when his flood of gratitude towards her has felt like love. When the girls were born, for example, and for those few days afterwards. Those days were amongst the happiest of his life.

For the past six months, he has had a lover: a white woman with a daughter who attends the same school as his girls. She is wealthy and lives alone on a hill that overlooks the old city centre of Johannesburg. Her house is made almost entirely of pale blue glass, and yet she remains to him opaque. They are dipping their toes into the forbidden, as one might try out a new drug.

He doesn't even particularly like his lover – as a person, that is – but at the time he didn't have the right words to repel her. Nor did he have the inclination, in spite of not quite liking her: he was too curious, even flattered, to turn away.

Is this really happening to me? he kept asking himself – and still asks himself. What is it that she sees in me? What is it that she sees when she looks at me? What have I become?

He has never been any good at being loved. He immediately suspects it and wants to belittle it, which means that he wants to suspect and belittle those who claim to love him — perhaps in order to preserve himself better. Yet with Noma and Nondumiso it has all been different: his daughters love him absolutely and he loves them back. Stepping away from them would be like walking away from the sun: he knows that he would quickly die without them.

So there is much that he can't tell the old woman. He knows she would want to boss him about, tell him what his duties were. She was always so good at telling others to face up to the truth, yet she could never see what was standing right there in front of her. Or was it simply that she never valued her own life enough to want to scrutinise it? In the days they still knew each other and he used to hang around this house, her own circumstances only ever earned the odd note of bemusement.

But there is one more thing he has to share with her before he leaves. He came here with a secret inside his jacket pocket — and now he takes it out, as one might extract an ancient and valuable book. She is watching him blankly, not knowing what's in store for her, not knowing how much he has wanted to hurt her with this wad of paper inside his pocket.

'Do you know what will happen to the farm after you are gone?' he asks her.

She looks at him with some surprise — as if to indicate he is veering off towards some unimportant topic.

'It's gone to some big land development company,' she says.

'Yebo, Madam,' he replies, speaking with a trace of his former irony. 'That is the company I work for.'

'You work for them?'

'Ye-bo.'

As he waves the folded map in the air, he's pleased to find the same expression on her face that she used to have whenever she was about to read his school report. He usually got five out of five for effort and an A for every subject except Afrikaans — which in those days the old woman liked to consider an additional accomplishment.

'How extraordinary.'

'Yebo, Madam,' he says.

He suspects she feels thrown by this latest trick, and perhaps a bit hurt, but now that he's started he can only carry on.

'I have come back here — yes. But not to reclaim the land that was taken from my people — no. I have come to establish what they call a gated community. For those who are fleeing the crime in the cities. The whites, mainly. And some Indians too. Actually, they're fleeing us blacks, but I think they prefer to call it "the crime".'

Thankfully, she chooses to laugh at this, and play along — and he finds himself smiling back, wolfish with a fresh appreciation of himself.

'Have you seen the latest plans?'

Without waiting for an answer — for he knows she can't possibly have seen the latest plans — he once again waves the innocuous-looking document at her. It now feels less like a school report and more like one of those poems he used to write, which always seemed unresolved somehow until he'd read them out to her. Even back then, he sensed the poems were inadequate, but it never seemed to matter: it was Looksmart she liked to marvel at — the visionary, not the vision.

'I have tried to avoid hearing too much about the plans,' she is saying. 'But now — well, I'd love to see them now!'

He pushes the wheelchair further away towards the door, picks up a trunk and places it before her. Then he adjusts the position of her standard lamp to get better light. He practically stretches his arms, clicks his knuckles, clears his throat. He forgets what the plans once meant: that they were intended to destroy all evidence of her forever; that they were an attempt to make coherent what he once called his hate. What seems to matter far more for the moment is that she apprehend the boldness of his thinking and award it a gold star.

'Come,' he says, unfolding and brushing out the map, 'come and see for yourself.'

She leans over and gazes at the map, full of admiring incomprehension. She appears to be looking for something amongst all those lines, her gaze moving in on details and then wandering off. When she speaks, however, it is with a surprising bitterness.

'What will happen to the house?' she says. 'After this, I hope they'll knock it down — brick by brick.'

It is the first time that evening that she's said anything that seems to speak for him — or aspire to speak for him — and yet, now that it happens, he finds he is no longer there where she expects him.

'The house? The house will be left on top of the hill. But we will cut down the trees to open things up a little. The place needs light, you see. A view of the Drakensberg: izintaba zoKhahlamba!'

'I don't know why we planted those trees,' she says. 'Only this morning, I was trying to think.'

He continues over her, suddenly wanting to get it all in: he's been repeating this speech in meetings with funders, architects, builders, but it always seemed to be falling on deaf ears — and only now does he realise that it was actually intended for her.

'Stylistically, this house has a vernacular value all of its own, which is why we have decided to reproduce it, a dozen times, with slight variations, all across the valley —'

As he moves away from the map and the pool of light, he feels his arms expanding outwards, his voice taking on the tone he reserves for meetings in that quietly humming office of his.

'The hills we know so well, they will be buried in pine plantations. The wetlands will be turned into dams for farming trout. And all those birds that surrounded me as a boy, that rainbow that always twittered — it will slowly fade, and one morning there will be silence.'

'How awful that sounds.'

'The hut I was born in, that will go too, along with all the farm buildings. Do you know how long it takes a machine to flatten a mud hut? It is the work of weeks to build it. You need earth from anthills for the foundations, cattle dung for the floors, uwatela for the walls and clay from the springs high up in the hills to fill the walls in. And the insika, the central pillar — that is selected by the men. You know we say you have to choose the insika carefully? The insika of the house is like the man of the house: it must be straight.'

'Indeed.'

'Well, all that work can be destroyed by a bulldozer before you can even cry for help.'

She smiles, almost laughs, apparently willing him onwards. An observer might think they were talking about a thing far away from themselves – another Science project, perhaps – not the land that runs like a fat immovable nerve through both of them.

'Ja, everything will go – everything except this house. This house will remain alone, but it will be transformed almost beyond recognition: there will be pale wooden floors, sliding doors, skylights, the veranda extended all around, and a turret structure will be added to the north wall to provide for what we call a vertical focus. Ah, Madam, you will see: we will whisk this whole place into something you could never imagine, not even in your wildest – nightmares!'

'I think it sounds – rather lovely.'

She almost laughs again, not quite seeming to believe in his tale. Maybe she thinks the trees are too thick, the piles of boxes too many, the weight in her bones too much for her to able to walk out of this house and close the door on it forever.

'We ought to have done all that years ago.'

'Open plan. Exactly!'

Patricia

It may be his dream house – this house transformed almost beyond recognition – but still it comes from her. Perhaps too much from her. Perhaps even today he's too attached to his pain – and all he's managing to do is reproduce it, with slight variations, all across the valley. But she can say none of this to him: now that he is finally talking in a way she can recognise, she's not about to undermine his momentum or diminish whatever it is he wants to tell her. And in spite of what she said about the house being knocked down, brick by brick, a part of her is also pleased by this evidence of his attachment to the house, her house, her father's house. It makes her feel that – amongst all the degradation – something good might also have come out of it all. They were not for nothing, her endeavours, her father's endeavours. A trace of their presence will remain here long after they are gone, and new houses will grow out of the earth where future generations might make a better job of things – and find that they are happy.

'How did you come to be involved in all this?' she says, wanting to keep him talking, keep him here — for after he has gone, there will be little to draw much comfort from.

'When the sale of the farm reached my ears, I wanted to make sure we would be involved in developing it.'

They both take a moment to ponder that word, smile at it.

'Well, I'm very pleased that it's you,' she says, 'who'll be doing it — the development.'

He inclines his head, never seeming to her more familiar, or more of a mystery.

'And by tomorrow,' she adds, 'we will be gone.'

'Yes.'

'And you will be able to clear yourself of everything — that's dead.'

This is more a provocation than a statement of fact, and he takes the bait, like the bad fisherman he once was.

'Dead?' he says, smiling, pensive. 'No, Madam. Now that I'm here — I don't know. I feel different about — all of this.'

For a moment she thinks he's going to say he loved her. She wants this more than anything, to be told she was loved by him — for a period, perhaps she was loved by him even more than his own mother was. But even if this were true, it is of course impossible for him to declare it: such expressions have never been their way.

'Tell me what happened to your mother,' she says. 'How's she keeping these days?'

'She's good — very well, in fact. She's been living with me for about fifteen years now. In my garden cottage — there in my house in Johannesburg.'

'That's very nice.'

She knows she probably sounds slightly put out, but she's also pleased he's looking after his mother — at the very least. It became his habit towards the end of his schooling to be unkind about her, and unkind to her. He seemed to be angry with his mother even before he was angry with Patricia, but Patricia never understood why. Was it safer to despise his mother first? Did he then resent Patricia because she had taught him to be ashamed of his mother?

'I'm pleased you're looking after her.'

'Well, what else do you expect?' he says – now the one to sound put out. 'Do you know, she still grows her own vegetables in the back garden. Can you believe that? A crop of mealies in the middle of Orange Grove!'

'I suppose she doesn't like to see all that wasted space.'

'That's true. She should be living somewhere out here. On a farm.'

'Then you ought to buy her one,' Patricia says.

Looksmart laughs, taking this as a joke, but she is being quite serious. She can't help but feel a bit disappointed in this scheme of his with the farm, even if the survival of her house might please her. He seems to think that the land, which is ultimately no more than a bit of wet bog between two hills, is the thing that needs to be worked on, whereas the only thing that needs working on is him: Looksmart himself.

'Your mother must be – very proud of you.'

'Oh yes.'

'She always has been proud of you. Since you first went to boarding school.'

'Don't I know it!'

She sees now that the tone regarding his mother survives in him still: it sounds like a faint echo, an almost undetectable remnant of his old self-loathing. He has the same need to diminish the earth he comes from, which is not so much the farm or even the country as it is his own flesh and blood.

'You know, when you first went away to that school,' she finds herself saying, 'your mother and I would often talk about you. We would sit at the kitchen table, the back door open, the flies bumping away as usual against the glass – and I would have to read out your school reports.'

'You would?'

'And although she couldn't read more than a word or two, your mother would carry those reports around in her overall pocket for days afterwards.'

None of this is quite true: Patricia has no memory of sitting with his mother in the kitchen, or even reading out his school reports, but she finds herself saying the words anyway, wanting to wake him up to his mother, and to Patricia herself, and to all the women who have ever loved him in his life.

'When I first went to school, my mother would look at me with strange eyes. With the same eyes she used when she looked at you. And by the time school was finished, I don't think I fitted anywhere. Not with her and certainly not with you.'

'Perhaps that's the price you had to pay,' Patricia says. 'Perhaps it's the price we all had to pay – each one of us.'

She has spent her whole life watching the things that have mattered the most to her leaving her. First her mother, whom she could barely remember, then little Rachel – and then her father, who simply fell down dead one day from a heart attack. In far more subtle ways, however, there has also been her husband, her lover and Looksmart. And this has extended to the farm itself: she has watched over the birth of each foal on the farm, charted its growth, treated its every ailment – and then sold it off the moment it was ready for independence. Nothing has ever come back to her. Everything around her – and much that has been happening in the country at large has only confirmed this – has only ever held evidence of loss or decay.

But recently she has also been observing all the new buildings starting up out of the earth, and the green crops of weeds appearing in the most improbable places. A few days ago, when she and Bheki were driving into the village, she noticed a cloud of yellow butterflies hovering around the weeds and spilling over across their path. Bheki drove on through them as though they weren't there, and neither of them said a word about it, but in that instant Patricia saw that there was an altogether different way of viewing the world: as an inexhaustible source of renewal and growth. And for a few minutes she was filled with what she could only have described as happiness.

'Do you think one day you will be able to come and visit?'

She doesn't believe he will as she says this. She doesn't even know if she would want him to: the future is still too tenuous a place for either of them to have any say in it.

'At your house by the sea?'

'Why not?' she smiles.

Even now, she can picture the house perfectly. It has a glass conservatory on the ground floor, looking across the lawn, which seems to end at the ocean, with nothing in between. Once she dreamed the whole house was made of glass, with everything transparent, so that every chair, every comb, every mote of dust could be seen from outside of it.

'We could take the old Rottweiler for a walk on the beach,' she says, a small bleak note already beginning to sound through her. 'We could throw sticks for it.'

'Ja,' he says, laughing – and seeming to understand her exactly, 'we could make it jump through hoops.'

She would like to tell him clearly that he was like her son – at least, the closest she ever got to having one – and that she will be lonely there, in her house by the sea. She would like to tell him that she wants him to visit her – even if it is just to humour a grey gogo with one or two marbles still rolling around inside her head.

He could even bring his wife and children. There will be so many rooms standing empty. And there will be the Victorian doll's house that once belonged to her grandmother. They could sit in the glass conservatory as her father's guests had once done, drinking gin, while the girls ran around the lawn, playing stuck in the mud. There was even a croquet set somewhere. The whole family could play after lunch, the better for drink, as her family had often done when she was a child.

But all of that feels immediately absurd. And anyway, children these days were forever playing on their phones and computers. Anything she would have to offer those two girls would look like nothing more than bits of old junk.

She would also like to admit that she will be afraid: she will be afraid tonight when the lights of the house are off, and she is surrounded by an altogether different darkness – but she also knows that he came here, at least in part, to achieve exactly this.

'I am pleased you have come,' she says instead, 'and I'm pleased that I've come to know you – a little.'

'You know nothing about me.'

He says this as though he wishes it weren't true, or is willing it not to be true.

'A few words, that is all.'

'Sometimes a few words can be enough – to show who a person is.'

She doesn't know what she means by this, for what kind of a person is he, exactly? It is more of an instruction, however, than a compliment – like his name. The golden thread that ran through him as a boy is shining through him still: even she can see that.

But she finds he is pacing the room again, with an old uneasiness.

'Ah, Madam,' he tells her. 'This is a strange land we live in. After all this time, you still want to be the mother. And me, I must still be something like your child. But that relationship – it can have no place in the future of this country.'

Richard

This is not his house because if it was his house the black girl would not be sitting on his bed like it was hers. She would not be sitting anywhere near him. She would be standing at the door. But he can also see that she intends him no harm. She has offered him tea in a china cup that he has encountered before and given him a blanket to sit inside. Her mistake is in thinking that she is like him. Or more specifically that he is like her. If only he could explain himself he could make her understand that he does not belong in this house. He belongs in some other house on the other side of the rain. But he doesn't have the words for it.

What's more, he's been through a lot. He feels wet and his hands have been bleeding and he doesn't know what it is he might have done. He is used to this feeling: that he has done a monstrous thing, but that the thing itself has gone off, like an article of clothing ripped away in the wind, and only the feeling it brought with it is left behind.

What have I done?

Is what he wants to know from her.

But as she says nothing he assumes he didn't speak it.

It's so difficult to know what is taking place. He is a man standing at the centre of an extraordinary dance. He doesn't know the steps for it. God knows, he is even deaf to the music. But all those around him seem to know exactly where to place their feet.

'Have I been here before?'

'Uke wafika la ngaphambilini.'

He draws comfort from the sound of her voice. Even though he knows that each of her words holds a lie inside it: he knows he has never been here before. But the lies don't surprise him. What surprises him is the confidence she has in her lies. And she seems to know before speaking that he won't have the words to refute them. Which suggests she knows him. Better than he knows her. Which suggests – he's prepared to admit – that she might not be lying to him after all: he may well have been here before.

He can see that thinking is useless. It only takes you back to where you started. Time might have passed, but you weren't the wiser. He would have to exercise far more cunning. If he has been here before it means he has left here before – and that he also knows how to get out of here. Of course there's the door, which is standing there where he expects it to be, which in itself is reassuring: all he has to do is use it. But the small woman has positioned herself between himself and the door in such a way that suggests she's anticipated this thought – and that on some other occasion he's already tried to escape.

Then he sees the spade leaned against the corner of the room, and he knows that he knows it and that it was he who took it. He wanted. He wanted to take it up to the grove on the. Where there are dark whisperings from under the earth. Little voice, looking for a way out of the earth.

Mother?

The drab-looking woman chooses not to hear this, or never hears it.

'Where did they bury you?'

He sees this time that his words seem to come out and hit on something. Because a part of the woman's face hardens. Perhaps she can see that he's not so useless after all.

'UMesis akafuni uye lapho.'

But he is not listening: he hears the dim sea-roar, the mountain black, and her voice calling out for him. Before the woman can think up another thing to move him away from his intent, he makes for the spade. But when he holds it in his hands he finds it is merely a stick, not a spade. But that is not the point, because like a hound he suddenly knows the route: there is a magnetic pull between himself and her heart, and he knows that he will find her if he doesn't pause to think.

Beauty

UBaas is gone when she emerges from the house: he is like a stone thrown into a river at night, swallowed up by a roar of darkness, so immediate and so complete that there is no point in going after it. So she trots back along the path towards the main house and uMesis, hoping all the way that Looksmart has satisfied himself with the direction his words have taken and gone back to where he came from.

There is no sign of Bheki in the kitchen either. She can only tell he was there from the angle of the chair where he sat. The angle of it tells her that he stood abruptly and went out, maybe upset with her for leaving without explanation. She doesn't know what his defection to Looksmart means, but she knows it is there: there is a new thing inside him, a new source of interest that he is not telling her about. But then he has never given her the important part of himself. She has always had to content herself with scraps.

Immediately on entering, she hears laughter from the front room. What new development is this? How can there be laughter after all that has been done? She has been expecting blood, violence, doom, not this peculiar sound of laughter. But the laughter also tells her that uBaas did not return to the house — that he is still out there, and still safe.

Richard

He can hear the rasping papery sigh of the trees before he reaches them. It is as if the last sighs of the dead have been gathered there, caught in a single breath, knowing nothing but an eternal vacancy. And at the centre of all this, she lies, her delicate intricate frame suspended inside the soft earth, her face a buried moon, alone and forgotten about by all but him.

He has been looking for this spot since before he can remember. But tonight the pull is clean and straight. He goes there immediately and his hands arrive at the rounded gravestone. He can feel moss around it, engulfing all the letters in the sandstone, and even now it seems about to disintegrate under his touch. Soon it will sink away into the land and be forever gone. There isn't much time. The girl in blue is out there tracking him. Wanting to draw him back to her makeshift houses. Wanting him to forget about this place, where the child lies alone in the earth. So he tears away at the mud and rock, yanking up bunches of grass, bits of splintered branch, a dead bird, a

handful of rotten fruit.
There is nothing there.
She has seeped back into the earth.
He fingers a twig, turns it in the dark.
And it gleams back at him, slim and firm as a chicken bone.

Patricia

The developers agreed to leave intact the bloodwood grove where Rachel lies. She liked to imagine they would place a bench there that looked across the valley towards the Kamberg and Giant's Castle. It is worrying, however, that Looksmart hasn't once referred to the site. In vain she looked for it on the map, but it was difficult to situate herself, with all those lines going off in every direction and each of those houses jostling for attention.

'What about my garden?' she finds herself saying. 'The roses. What will happen to them after we've gone?'

'I will make sure we keep them exactly as they are.'

She can see him wanting to placate her – and she knows he is probably lying about the roses. In the morning, she will have to ask Bheki to dig the coffin up. There is a small blue trunk still lying empty that should do the trick. She isn't about to leave her child alone on the hill, and wonders how she ever thought she could.

'Don't worry, Madam,' he is saying. 'The bulldozers will not dig them up.'

'Thank you.'

She smiles at him, feeling easier. She will take Rachel away with her tomorrow and have her buried at the old St Thomas's church – alongside her parents.

As for Looksmart, she finds she likes him for his lies far better than she likes him for his truths.

'But don't forget to deadhead them.'

'And prune them every July,' he smiles. 'Ja, I haven't forgotten. You have to cut them right down.'

She laughs again – at the wit of him, and the wit of them, which is the closest they have ever come to expressing their affection.

'You have to be quite brutal about it,' she says.

'And if you over-water them, the leaves will suddenly turn yellow and fall off.' Now he is laughing back at her. 'Do you remember when I did that to the ones in the pots? All along your veranda – I made your roses to go yellow. They looked like they were dead. You remember that?'

It is the first thing they can both recall equally, clearly, like something that happened only yesterday.

'Yes!'

'You tried your best to be nice about it, but hell – you were cross!'

Richard

He is standing in the front garden with a rock in his hands the size of a human skull. Only far heavier. But he is satisfied. Far more satisfied than he has felt all night. At last he has found the house, precisely as he expects it. The gate, which his fingers unlatch without a thought, the stretch of lawn, the solid fact of the house itself. When the dog Ethunzini sees him, she squirms in the shadows exactly as he anticipates, making her basket creak. And the front door right there where it ought to be, with the usual light coming at him from the place of his wife.

He barely registers the silver car still standing under the tree and has no ears for the voices coming from inside the room. With a nudge of his muddied slipper he pushes open the door and steps in. And what he sees next is the most unlikely event of the night: a black man wearing a suit. What's more, laughing with his wife. Engaged in what looks remarkably like happiness. Like young lovers. Yet hardly that, because there sits his wife, large and round and grey and not even seeming to see him. Then he realises that she has indeed seen him and is putting off the moment of seeing him – if only for another second.

What is going on?

'What have you done?'

Are the words that are said.

As the man in the suit moves off she tries to stand. Her whole body is twisted towards him, wanting to lurch at his rock.

'What is that in your hands, Richard?'

'I saw the house burning. As I was digging in the dark. But we're still here, aren't we?'

'Yes.'

'I thought something terrible had happened. The girl wailing in the wind. I though at last. We'd all be dead. But we aren't dead, are we?'

'We are not dead.'

The man makes a sound like laughter that is not laughter.

'And who the hell is this?'

'The surveyor.'

'The?'

'He works for the land development company. He was about to leave.'

Patricia

'Beauty!'

She knows that Beauty is in the kitchen, listening. Earlier she heard the flyscreen squeak open and shut, indecisively, like a person sitting down on a tired mattress and then immediately deciding to stand up.

A part of her wants whatever will happen to happen. Yet she calls for the girl out of a sense of duty, a duty to the role that has been left to her. She has always been the mediator between these two, and for once she wants that to stop. But still she calls out for the girl, with a steadiness to her tone that is designed to suggest to the two men that nothing irreparable has happened yet.

'Beau-ty!'

Looksmart

The old man is walking towards him, wearing a pink anorak and a pair of sorry-looking slippers. He is carrying a rock, but he is still the same man. Half the size and all the colour washed out of him, but still the same man. His hair is stuck to his face and there is a smear of red mud across his mouth, but his eyes have the same pale blue deadness about them, like the eyes of a drowned man who has already spent a week underwater.

He advances, slippery with guile, almost expecting to be hit.

'Isn't it a bit late for this?' he says.

'It is never too late for this.'

It's odd how little thought he has given this man. It was usually only the old woman he would contemplate. The man was less contentious, easier to categorise, not so difficult to dismiss. But he really does look like he stepped out of a swamp: the body clammy and bloodless and the absurd anorak smeared with filth.

Looksmart finds himself stepping forward, his hand held out like a gun. The other man takes it rather grudgingly, looking like someone who has just lost a game of cards.

'So you do not recognise me?'

'Should I?'

'I am Phiwayinkosi Ndlovu, Gatsheni, boya benyathi busongwa, busombuluka zidlekhaya ngoba ziswele abelusi – Ngonyama! But I think you knew me once as Looksmart.'

The man blinks, taking this tirade in his stride. He is bemused, even. A man who has just lost everything but is still able to appreciate a good joke.

'Looksmart. And where is it we met?'

'Right here. On this farm. Some years ago.'

The man recoils slightly, snarls inwardly, as if he has just been burnt.

'I never heard of any Looksmart. What kind of a name is that?'

'It is a name. Like Baas is a name.'

'And what are you doing wearing a suit? Did someone die?'

Looksmart can feel Patricia's gaze on him. He doesn't have to look at her to know what she wants from him: to walk away, to leave this man to his ignominious fate.

And in that moment he has never imagined himself to be so strong.

'I came to shed a bit of light,' he says.

'Well you remind me of my Uncle Pete,' the old man says. His hostility merely turns out to have been another kind of joke – suggesting that everything, in the end, can be reduced to nothing more than a joke.

'Have you ever met my Uncle Pete?'

'I haven't had that pleasure. No.'

The old man steps forward and places his rock on the mantelpiece, next to Looksmart's keys and the apple. He picks up the apple and starts to eat it, the skin jiggling about like a stretched spring.

'Let me tell you a little story about my Uncle Pete,' he says. 'The last time I saw him, he was lying here, on this carpet, wearing a suit. Poor bugger had a food allergy. Peanuts. So he says to me, "Richard, I have something very serious to confess." "Don't worry Pete," I tell him, "you get it off your chest." So he tells me, "Over the past years," he says, "whenever I've come to stay, I've been going over to your daughter's room at night, and I've been holding her down, and I've been fucking her."'

'Your what?' Patricia says.

'Your daughter,' he says.

'But you do not have a daughter,' Looksmart says.

'Are you going to listen to this story or what?'

When neither of them speaks, the old man carries on, once again in a way that implies the moment of tension was no more than a joke: 'Anyway, so I tell Pete. "Listen, Pete. It's all in the past. Let's forgive and forget. Right? We'll put it all behind us and carry on. But Pete," I tell him, "now that we're deciding to confess and all, I've got something to say to you. I'm the one who put the peanuts in the sherry trifle!"'

The old man is about to start laughing when he is overtaken by a fit of coughing. No one moves to help him.

'Well,' says Looksmart, 'I'm glad I never met this – Uncle Pete.'

The old man turns again with that inward snarl towards Looksmart, but Looksmart doesn't move. He smiles, pretending that the man in front of him only amuses him now.

'Do you know there was a time I would have had you whipped?'

Under the gaze of Patricia, Looksmart wipes the mud off his hands onto the other man's anorak. He thinks that he is going to kill him. Everyone thinks it. Yet the old Baas is doing nothing to defend himself. He seems to be offering himself up, almost to prove a private point.

'Old man,' Looksmart tells him, 'there is nothing you can tell me that I don't already know.'

The old man looks thrown for a moment: perhaps he was expecting something more violent, more overt – something he could actually grasp.

'Do you know what I'm going to do?' Looksmart continues. 'I'm going to leave you to your wife.'

He turns to the old woman and tries to smile at her, but finds he can't quite achieve it. The old man has ruined all that, as he always did.

'Good night, Patricia.'

'From tomorrow – a new start?'

A lingering sense of decency makes him shrug this off.

'I'm a heavy bull, with three bellies to feed. The rest of my life belongs to my family. And the manager of the bank.'

Richard has taken a step forward. He is swaying slightly, looking drunk: 'A real man isn't scared of a bit of debt.'

Patricia is leaning forward in her chair, an expression of pain pulling at the side of her mouth.

'One day you will come?' she says. 'We will go down to the beach – throw sticks?'

He decides on a final lie: 'Of course.'

'What on earth are you two going on about?'

'Uhambe kahle, Madam,' Looksmart says, picking up his keys. 'Don't worry, I will let myself out.'

Bheki

Bheki sees him stepping out of the house and into the wet night. Looksmart hesitates on the stoep, maybe wondering if he really is leaving the house or is only acting it. He looks around like a man with nowhere left to go. Then he appears to remember the dog Ethunzini. Bheki can see the dark shape of the dog, watching the other man as if it has always known him. Looksmart's body changes when it faces the dog, looking like he is ready to attack or be attacked. But the dog does nothing. It stares back at Looksmart, sighs and rests its head on the edge of the basket.

Patricia

There is no change in the room after he has left it. Richard still stands there like someone expecting an important telephone call, and Patricia remains in her chair, rather like someone who's not. But they are both listening to the progress of the man who has left them. The front door closes behind him – a thin, rattling door that has never felt substantial enough – and the man pauses on the concrete of the stoep. She knows the dog is there, yet it makes no sound and the man does not seem to step towards it. Perhaps she is asleep, or dead. It is unlike Ethunzini not to make any sound, even a whimpering of pleasure at the emergence of a familiar figure from the house.

'Who did he say he was? He said he knew me. He said we'd met before, I think.'

She is looking at the rock. Although covered with orange mud, she recognises it: an almost perfectly round piece of pink basalt flecked with white
that her father brought to her from a river under Giant's Castle, around
the time she and Richard first met. The rock lived on the front stoep until
Rachel's death, and then one summer afternoon Patricia carried it to the
grave and placed it on a mound of moss, where it has remained until tonight.

'Rachel,' she says.

'Do not say that name in this house.'

Richard's clarity of feeling on the subject of Rachel usually comes as a
surprise to Patricia, but now she barely considers him.

'What did you do to her?' she says. 'Please don't tell me you tried to dig
her up.'

Richard is looking cowed, but it is an expression he was probably born
with, so it tells her nothing new. She knows that he would have found it
almost impossible to find the gravesite in the dark, let alone recall what he
wanted to do once he got there, but tonight he has brought in the rock. It
sits there glistening on the mantelpiece like a freshly laid egg.

'Where did you get that rock? Tell me, Richard.'

'There was nothing there,' he says.

'Nothing where, exactly?'

'I couldn't find it.'

'She's not an it, Richard – she's our child.'

'It wasn't a child. It was a joke. She was trying to provoke me, that's all.
The lying bitch.'

It is his way these days to hide himself in obscurity the moment she gets
close to him. Usually she lets him, and feels slightly relieved. But not tonight.

'Say her name, Richard.'

'What?'

'Say her name: Rachel.'

'No.'

'Okay – then say Grace.'

'What?'

'Say the name Grace. Grace! Say it.'

'What are you trying to – say?'

'Grace.'

'What are you trying to do to me? Didn't the doctors say I was to avoid all stress?'

She gets to her feet, her anger stronger than any pain, and takes one step towards him. He looks more frightened at this than at anything she might have said: he has misjudged her: she can actually walk!

'I could see very well that you recognised him, Richard. It was an act. Is that what this is? Is all of this – an act?'

He steps back, perhaps imagining she is about to strike him. And maybe she is. If she can get close enough, if only she can get at his neck.

'You aren't half as mad as you pretend to be, are you?'

He blinks at her like a bird. A crow, perhaps – incredulous. He looks almost merry, seeing her walking again, like it's something farcical. She on her own two feet at last. Then he takes a step towards her, looking intent on striking her back, full of his old cowardly spite.

'Of course I know Looksmart. I said at the time it was a mistake – sending him to that school, giving him ideas above himself. But you didn't want to listen to me – and you never have. The only man you've ever listened to is your father.'

'That's because he was the only man ever worth listening to.'

'And what did you create in the end? Looksmart! He looks like a fucking twat to me. In his fucking suit.'

'Well that fucking suit now owns this place, Richard.'

'So what's he going to do with it? Open a shebeen?'

Richard turns away and tries to laugh, but he's too dried up inside, and there's no laughter left – just a vacant space that echoes strangely.

'Tell me, Richard. You tell me what you did to Grace.'

'It was a lie, designed to upset me. I never believed a word of it. I never believed we could have made – that.'

'What in God's name are you talking about?'

'There's nothing more to say about it. It was a trick, a twist, a knife in my back. How many times do I have to say it?'

He's almost weeping with bewilderment and self-pity, and she finds she's too tired to carry on standing – so she finds the arms of the chair behind her, and lowers herself back into place.

The pain will come later. Tonight, when she is trying to sleep. She will have to take double her pills. All of her pills, perhaps. How glorious it would be not to have to wake up. It would be better to spend her last night on the farm. No one has ever really believed in Durban anyway. Which might be why they have never quite managed to pack.

'Don't you want to give yourself some peace?' she asks eventually.

He seems to consider this, but about as seriously as one might consider the choice between tea or coffee.

'No,' he says, as if he knows he's speaking for both of them – and knows she will never have any peace.

'There was no name,' he adds. 'No name for it.'

'No name for what, Richard?'

He regards her more clearly than he has in months. For a moment, the old Richard, the first one she met, appears to have returned – the one with nothing to hide.

'You don't actually know, do you?' he says.

'I know all I need to know. You unleashed the dog. You murdered her.'

'Oh – that.'

He turns from her and almost laughs with disappointment, and some relief, and a note of contempt.

'Is that all?'

'Christ. Isn't that enough?'

'She was – lying.'

'Oh God. Don't you feel any remorse?'

'For what? For you? But I've never done anything to you.'

'For her, Richard. For Grace!'

'Are you mad?'

He himself has never looked madder, more dangerous and lost.

'I can't even – look at you,' she says at last.

He turns away again. Doing her the favour of concealing his face. And when he speaks it is with his child's voice.

'Who are you anyway? What makes you the judge? All puffed up. Looking down at me. You putrid cunt.'

She shouts now as she hasn't for years, wanting the whole house, the whole valley, the whole country, to hear her: 'Go – leave – get out – get out of my sight!'

She has to concentrate on drawing air into her body when he is gone. It is a technique she has employed through the ages to digest her rage at him. Only tonight there is more rage in her than any body should ever be asked to contain. There is a broken feeling inside her chest, like a sharp pipe has quietly snapped, and is veering this way and that, tearing at her most vital organs.

Her gaze then settles on the mantelpiece and she sees the rock: he was here. The rock exists, so he exists: everything that happened really did happen. And he must have left no more than a minute ago, maybe two: there is still time to catch him up.

'Looksmart?'

She says the name quietly, testing out the dimensions of the name in the room.

'Looksmart.'

Now she says it with more conviction, pushing herself up and out of the chair once more. She sees the wheelchair standing by the door where Looksmart left it.

Ignoring the shards of glass twisting down her back and into her hips, she shuffles towards the wheelchair. She wonders why the Alsatians never barked when Looksmart emerged from the house – and it takes another pace to relearn once again that the dogs are dead.

'Beauty!'

She curses Beauty for never being there at her first call, for always providing another source of effort. She imagines the girl sitting in the kitchen, hearing the lack of dogs, the departing car, the voice of her employer, and still deciding to hang back, waiting for the moment to pass, so she could appear when it was too late and Looksmart was gone and everything would be as it was again – even though nothing ever would be.

'Beau-ty!'

She reaches the wheelchair somehow, sits and turns towards the corridor. As she arrives at the front door – which stands ajar thanks to Richard – she sees the two burning coals of Looksmart's rear lights. They swing away from her, then rise and descend with the contours of the dirt road.

'Looksmart!'

She raises her hand, halfway between bidding him farewell and summoning him back. Even at this decisive moment she can't say exactly what it is she wants from him. All she wants is to bring him back, to continue the conversation, even if they talk about nothing of consequence, like a film he might have liked, the subjects at school his daughters were good at, the health of his mother, a seemingly insignificant fact about his wife – but she knows she will never know anything more about him. The two coals sway away and flicker into the bloodwoods, around the rubble where the stables once stood, and into the night.

'Mesis?'

Beauty has been standing beside her throughout Looksmart's departure, watching him go – and Patricia can hear the false sympathy in her voice, the note of relief.

'I wanted to – thank him.'

She doesn't know why she says this or what there is to thank him for. She hasn't fully comprehended what might have happened, or what it might mean for them.

But Beauty is already turning her away, guiding the wheelchair back into the house – a ruined warship being brought back into harbour.

'Kulungile, Mesis,' she says. 'He will understand.'

Beauty

She seems to get heavier every day. It's a mystery, as she hardly eats much more these days than uBaas. Yet her bones are old and heavy, and full of a long and difficult life – and the bones of uBaas are light as a child's, like a boy with all his days still ahead of him.

When she takes the arm of uMesis, she hardly appears to notice.

'Kulungile, Mesis,' she says. 'He will understand.'

But these are only words, passing by like bees in the air, with neither of them paying them much attention.

Instead of taking her back to the room with all its boxes, she leads her through her bedroom and into the bathroom. She yanks the grubby string that ignites the florescent light, and the room stutters into life. In that ghostly blue daze, uMesis looks colourless and already dead, her dress hanging off her body like a table cloth thrown across a large white rock.

Beauty has always liked this room, with its sink stained with decades of dripping and its huge awkward taps, and the metal standing bath that takes half a morning to fill up and that hasn't been used for many years now because of uMesis's back. It is a bathroom for people with a large vision of life, who are not afraid of wasting water or using up gas. Occasionally she will bring uBaas in here for a bath — or run one for herself when uBaas is asleep and uMesis is out.

When uMesis has arrived at the toilet, she steps outside and closes the door behind her. She hears the echoing dribble of uMesis's urine and enters after the appropriate pause to stretch up to the metal chain and flush. The whole house seems to cough into life as the brownish water swirls through the toilet and they turn and shuffle across to the bed. She knows uMesis doesn't like to speak at such times as this. She is embarrassed by Beauty's presence, and so it is Beauty's duty to make herself as small as possible, so that uMesis can pretend she isn't there.

After they've reached the bed, she takes the nightgown from under the pillow, thinking how sad it is to be doing such things for the last time in this house. She has been telling herself that she is looking forward to going down to Durban, to that house by the sea, with its pale yellow air and its ships honking across the harbour — as described by uMesis — but now she is not so sure about Durban, or the meaning of Durban. Perhaps she will be doing nothing more there than treading the same path, but in a different place.

She pulls back the sheets and uMesis sits. When Beauty has undone all the buttons, the dress falls away. UMesis seems to be listening to a faraway sound — like a car engine fading off into the night.

When she has fed uMesis's arms into the night dress and done up the new set of buttons, uMesis falls back into her pillows and stares up at the light, which has a pale pink lampshade filled with dead bugs. Beauty is reminded again of that overgrown baby bird: wide-eyed, feathery, abandoned, lost.

'You must try to sleep,' Beauty tells her. 'We have a long day tomorrow.'

'Yes — goodnight.'

Then Beauty switches off the light, closes the door and continues down the corridor to check on uBaas.

Five

Patricia

She draws back the curtains to reveal the mist. It lies there as it did before, filling the valley and invading every cupboard of the house. The bloodwoods are also present, like attendant ghosts awaiting instructions. Little do they know how soon they will be levelled. The mottled grey boles flecked with lichen will soon be torn into by a row of spinning teeth, and the fresh red wood will lie exposed: the shock of colour that has always been their secret.

She dreamed all night again about the earthmovers, but this time it was the Durban house under attack, with all of them inside it – and the yellow and black machines were more like locusts, swaying their forelegs, their mandibles moving, with tiny men sitting inside their eyes, which glittered like black diamonds. The venerable façade of the old house swayed and came down with a crash, and the machines moved in, over the crushed glass of the conservatory, their long jagged limbs foraging through the rubble, trying to get at them.

But if the bloodwoods are still there, it means that Rachel will be there too, safe in her grave on the hill. Suddenly she understands the Ancient Egyptians: it wasn't that they wanted to take the world they knew with them into the afterlife – they probably suspected, like most of us, that death was the end of it all – no, it was far more likely that what they wanted was to protect their belongings from the reach of others. They wanted to keep that which was sacred to them close to them. For objects know nothing about loyalty: they know they will never be owned by anyone. Like the body of Rachel, they had to be protected by those who understood their value, for they had no ability to value themselves.

'Beau-ty!'

She has been listening to the sounds inside the house since before dawn. Richard cried out at one point – a wheezing gasp like a fox – but she left him to his bad dreams or wild imaginings. There was also the sound of leathery scratchy feet marching along the iron roof – the rock pigeons waiting for the sun to come up – and then, just before dawn, the creaking of the drongos, followed by the hadedahs and their eternal squabble in the trees. By the time Beauty finally entered the house – with the discreet squeak of the flyscreen, never to be heard again – the first rumble of the earthmovers had already started up.

For the first time since Patricia can remember, Beauty appears at the bedroom door without a second call. She looks different today because she is wearing a dress. It is a dress Patricia has seen her donning for funerals: a simple cotton garment with small blue flowers. Forget-me-nots, perhaps. But her feet are as bare as usual.

'How are you this morning, Beauty?'

'I am fine, Mesis.'

'Good. Did you sleep well?'

'Not so good, Mesis.'

'No – not so good,' Patricia says, smiling.

They gaze at each other, but Beauty's body – out of habit, out of duty – is still leaning in the direction of Richard, as no one has checked up on him yet. It occurs to Patricia that they could stop checking up on him altogether. They could get in the car and drive off to Durban and leave him here on the farm, to dodge the builders and find a comfortable porcupine hole to nest in at night. He could probably get by on earthworms and brambleberries. He could be a parting gift to Looksmart.

'I have been thinking about the grave,' she says.

'Yebo, Mesis.'

Beauty, who often apprehends her thoughts better than she does, seems to know which grave she is talking about.

'I would like Bheki to go there and take her out. Could you go with him? I want you to make sure everything's – okay.'

Beauty doesn't flinch at this latest task, or if she does, she gives no sign of it.

'Yebo, Mesis.'

'He can put the coffin in that blue trunk. The one on the floor of the old tack room. He must position the coffin inside, and then surround it with earth. I don't want it to move about. It has to be properly supported, all right?'

Beauty inclines her head and says nothing, her eyes moving as she rehearses the task.

'He can use one of the old combination locks to lock it up,' she continues. 'I've been thinking – she should be buried where my parents are. At the old St Thomas's church. I was married there and christened there – and both my parents are buried there too.'

The oats is waiting for her in the kitchen as usual, but today the silver sugar bowl has been packed away and there is only a brown packet of sugar with a teaspoon inside it. The milk is in a chipped pale yellow jug that Patricia doesn't recognise, and the milk is still warm from the cow that made it – the cow that will go to the family of Bheki's wife in Msinga Top.

Patricia stands in the kitchen, inhaling the smell of dank cupboards and leaking gas. Now that the room is bare, and there is nothing left in it to see but the room itself, she realises that it looks like a poor person's kitchen. Since their arrival, she has not upgraded the kitchen. She has never upgraded anything. She simply accepted the kitchen and the rest of the house as a fact, as one would accept a tree on the horizon – a thing that was already itself and didn't need further intervention. If anything, she has wanted to preserve the simplicity of the house. Its simplicity used to strike her as a form of honesty. Like her father, it was unashamedly itself – and it asked the same of all those who passed through it. She loved the way the little gas burners above the baths and the kitchen sink started up only when you needed warm water. And the way the wood-fuelled AGA heated one half of the house – the south-facing half – through the winter. Until fairly recently, they still had that wind-up phone that connected them to the operator in the village – a solitary forgettable woman called Miss Pembroke, who must have listened in on every exchange between herself and John Ford.

Yes, Patricia has liked to feel a bit medieval in this house. When she was pregnant, she found herself making big stews for herself and her husband, throwing in any vegetable or herb that was currently available from the garden, and hunks of freshly cut meat from the farm – usually lamb. The prospect of a fecund and varied life still lay ahead of them and, back then, Patricia imagined that this funny diminished kitchen – no more than a corner of the house, ill-lit from its high south-facing windows – would provide the heart of the house.

Soon afterwards, they failed their first test following the death of Rachel. And they had failed just about every other test since. Only now can she see how ignorant she was: because she had always had a gracious life, she imagined it would continue, and that grace was a characteristic you were born with. She never knew – and was never told – that grace had to be worked for and protected. Her so-called grace may only ever have come from her father – by association – ending as soon as she went off with Richard.

She once said to John Ford that it was not Richard himself she wanted back then, it was the idea of a life that she thought would come through him – along with the novelty of sex, which she later realised she could have found with almost any man.

As she looks at the room's worn surfaces and the dead flies along the windowsill, she knows that she chose this, that she helped to create it. Even now she does not understand the source of her abiding apathy, but she has sometimes wondered whether it was her father's love that ruined her, for everything else since then has been a bit of a disappointment.

From deep inside the house, she hears Richard crying out again, followed by the murmured reassurances of Beauty, who is probably trying to get him dressed. She sprinkles sugar over the oats and lets it melt before adding milk. All those years – she thinks – and Beauty never said a word: not about Richard, not about Grace, not about any of it. And there she is, still dressing him, feeding him, wiping his arse – instead of doing what Looksmart wanted to do, and cutting out his heart.

'Can you tell me where the bathroom is?'

Richard is standing at the doorway wearing his blue pyjama shirt and nothing else. His genitals are like an old peach withered into itself and fluffy with mould. He is almost luminous, standing in the sunlight. He is made of white dust. If she blew in his direction, he might disappear. What did Looksmart call him again? A moth – yes – without any substance left. She knows now that Looksmart's way of looking at him will be – at least in part – her way of looking at him.

'Come and eat your oats, Roo. We have a long journey ahead of us.'

'And where are we off to, exactly?'

Beauty appears with his corduroys and stares at her, looking helpless. But she is far from helpless: she is simply self-conscious in front of Patricia: she can't work with Richard as she usually does under Patricia's gaze.

'We are going to the sea.'

Patricia says this as she continues to eat her oats. She sees from the corner of her eye Richard stepping obediently into his pants. She doesn't ask why he isn't being given any underpants.

'But I don't know how to swim,' he says.

'Of course you do: you can't have forgotten that.'

Beauty pulls back his chair and he sits.

'Well what would you know about it?' he says – eyeing the sugar and then helping himself to far too much.

Bheki

He is standing under the bloodwoods with Beauty. There is a faint hissing, like the pressure being released from a tyre, even though the air is almost still. It is also warmer today. The mist is slowly shifting. The sky will be clear by the time they are ready to leave.

Something has been busy near the grave. As recently as last night. The black earth has been churned up here and there – randomly, as a porcupine might do – but the small headstone and slight mound where Rachel lies have been left untouched. Then he sees it's one of the dog graves that was dug up. He knows this because he dug the grave and buried the dog himself: a Rhodesian ridgeback called Jess that was always said to be too soft. A white bone gleams in the mud, wiped or licked clean by the animal that unearthed it.

The earth is soft but the coffin is buried deep – deeper than expected – and it requires some effort to reach it. The wood looks slightly slimy, almost black, but the coffin still seems to be intact. Moving with deliberation, he clears the earth away until the coffin stands alone, restored to its shape – and then he gets to his feet and stretches and they both regard it.

He and Beauty have hardly spoken since they came out here. She seems to be sulking with him for some reason. He never spends much thought on her moods, for they are as mysterious as the weather that comes in from the mountains: unpredictable, changeable, brooding, dramatic.

He knows that she is in love with him. Everyone actually knows it. Over the years he's been teased enough about it by the other workers on the farm – even, once or twice, by the Madam herself. And the truth is that he has quite liked being loved by her. He has even – in the most subtle and unspoken ways – encouraged it. He has always preferred the world with Beauty in it, even if he has also known he will never touch her in the way she would like him to. Before his marriage – which happened late – he had even gone so far as to contemplate the thought of Beauty: she was so loyal, so absolute, so trusting in spite of everything that had happened around her. If he was with her, he wouldn't have to think, or try to please her: she would be pleased enough just to have him. But the idea of his flesh on her flesh – in spite of her relative youth – has always sent alarm bells through him.

When he finally decided to marry Phumelele, Beauty barely spoke to him for a year. She wanted him to see how well she could do without him, but the ferocity of her decision, and the consistency with which she carried it out, only confirmed the extent to which she loved him still. The birth of Bongani and the strangeness that came with him gave her an excuse to come back to him: she could pity him for the child, and carry on loving him as a nun likes to love a saint.

So he doesn't have the heart to tell her that he will not be staying in Durban. He will take the old people down and help them to settle in, but as soon as the Madam has found another driver, he will return to work here on the farm. Looksmart has promised him a job and he has said he will send Bongani to a special school, so that his disabilities will not hold him back. Looksmart said it was the time for black people to help each other. That the time of getting help from the whites is finished. And he agrees with this. He thinks it is time he walked away from this distasteful dance he has been engaged in for so long: where he has to disturb the grave of a child just because the Madam has decided it.

Beauty will die inside when she hears about his defection, but she will have to endure this as she has endured all else. As it happens, he has come to see the Madam and Beauty as two sides of the same thing, and he would like to kill off his feelings for both of them. He has carried the pain of them for long enough.

Without speaking, he bends down and passes his hands underneath the box, and Beauty copies him. It is heavy with wet. Spreading their four hands as wide as they can underneath it, they draw the box upwards as gently as they can. It wobbles slightly but retains its shape.

He can still picture the moment they put the box in the earth. Then it had been the colour of a horse chestnut, with a nutty glow inside it, carefully varnished. To the small boy holding onto the clothes of his father – part of the gathering of workers observing the ceremony from a distance – it seemed almost a pity to put such a beautifully crafted object into the earth, where no one would ever admire it. But now he is grateful for the quality of the wood.

The Madam was standing very still when the workers finally stepped forward to bury the child. She threw flowers into the little hole, but no earth. It is said that she only wept later, when she was alone in the house. And the servants of the time never disturbed her grief: they would bring her tea and something to eat only when she had exhausted it. Then the Madam would devour whatever was given her without seeming to notice it: she could eat a whole cake, or a chicken, or a pot of soup – pouring in bits of cut-up buttered toast and a jug of cream.

It is also said that the only period the Madam was happy was when the boy Looksmart was in her house. Bheki recalls seeing the boy walk in through the front door like he'd always lived there – and how he'd admired the boy for it. Because the boy expected the best of the Madam, and thought nothing of her sorrow, he managed to provide a place where she could laugh again and be a better person for a while. After he went, Bheki continued to be her driver, but all the words that could ever have been spoken between them already felt finished. There was nothing left to do but drive up and down the driveway in the same car, buy the same food from the same shop, and occasionally visit the old umlungu, John Ford.

The coffin fits neatly into the blue trunk. They gaze at it for a while before he bends to scoop and pack the earth around it – so that it won't slide around inside. He even pats a layer of earth over the top of the coffin – picking away the odd wayward frond or twig – so that it can once again be out of sight. Then Beauty locks the trunk with the combination lock she has been carrying in her pocket. He knows that only she and the Madam know the numbers for opening it.

The Madam is waiting for them in her wheelchair in the sunlight of the stoep. She watches their progress across the lawn. Both of them are wearing the expressions of those who know they are carrying a dead child. This is not just a bale of teff. They show her how respectful they are feeling, even though they are feeling it. Inside the house, the phone is ringing, but no one moves to answer it. And there is no sign of the Baas.

High above them, the weaverbirds are attending to their nests. And from the other side of the trees an earthmover is groaning towards them. There is nothing unusual in the air, yet with the arrival of the dead child, everything has changed: for the first time Bheki begins to understand that these people will be leaving this place for good.

Patricia

The telephone continues to ring as she follows the coffin into the house. Not knowing what else to do with it, Bheki and Beauty place the coffin before the dead fireplace, at the foot of the mantelpiece. The round stone Richard brought in the previous evening is still sitting there, the orange clay having since dried into a pale terracotta grey. As the phone is still ringing when the other two are gone, she wheels across to pick it up.

'Is that Patricia Wiley?'

'It is.'

'This is Mrs Bell from the school.'

'Oh, hello.'

There is no reason for Mrs Bell to call. There is a high anxiety in her voice. Patricia asks her what has happened.

'It's John Ford. I'm afraid there's been an – accident.'

'Is he dead?'

'I'm so sorry.'

'Murdered?'

'I don't – no. I don't think so.'

Patricia now asks the question that passed through her – for some reason – the moment she heard Mrs Bell's ridiculous voice.

'Are you saying that John has killed himself?'

'We – well, it looks like that may be the case.'

'At his house?'

'Yes.'

Mrs Bell also knew about their affair. For years, she was the one who did the necessary covering up. But it doesn't quite explain why Patricia is being called now.

'Would you like me to go over there?' she says.

'I'm afraid the police have – requested it.'

'Why is that?'

'Because he left a note.'

'I understand,' she says – understanding nothing. 'I'll be right over.'

She puts down the phone and stares at the blue tin trunk: it seems she'll be able to commune with her child properly only when she herself is dead.

She finds the letter in the cubbyhole where she stuffed it and is about to open it when she feels Bheki's hungry gaze on her. So instead she pushes it into her handbag.

'It's John Ford,' she says. 'Apparently he died last night.'

Bheki nods and says nothing – in a way that suggests Beauty has already told him the gist of it.

They drive away from the house in silence, Patricia hardly seeing the farm and its churned up ruin of earth and rock. The landscape is still lost in the mist. There is only the car, following the dirt road, with nothing but a void at either end of it.

To a degree that she would not have only a day before, she feels herself responsible for this latest event. Her crime, it seems – with Richard, with Looksmart, and now with John – has been a lack of imagination. She thought it was enough to sit in her house on the hill, thinking her thoughts, measuring her days, issuing only the most necessary instructions, but Looksmart's visit has changed all that: simply from the direction of his gaze, which could pick its way through a million moments in her life and bring to her attention one or two whose consequences had endured – and endured horribly. It is a gaze she will now be able to apply to herself, at her leisure – and she will be even more effective than he, since she has access to each of her decisions and their effects.

As they labour along the road, the image of the black puppy keeps finding its way back into her head: the way it would run along the fence of the dog-run after the girls going towards the dairy, stumbling over its paws, while she sat back and laughed at it.

There is an ambulance, a police car and a small yellow Toyota standing at odd angles in the gravel driveway. The driver of the ambulance is sitting on a rock in front of a bed of blooming agapanthus, smoking a cigarette, looking towards the sky – perhaps willing the sun to come out. Bheki parks in the usual place, extracts the walker from the boot and opens the door for her. He does not enter after her, but turns and walks away from the house, perhaps off to cadge a cigarette.

John's tobacco smoke is still lingering in the curtains and the furniture of the house. His fragrant exhalations. The golf clubs are stacked against the wall, each of the clubs peering out, eager for use. She stops in the corridor near the entrance to the sitting room, wondering where to go, listening out for voices – but all is still. Perhaps the body's already in the ambulance. All she's clear about is that she doesn't want to have to look at it.

'Hello?'

It's odd to call for someone in John's house that isn't John. She feels his vacancy answering back at her. Then she hears a murmur coming from the bedroom, a room she hasn't been to since – she doesn't want to think about it.

A young woman appears, surprisingly pretty. Not at all like the police officer she might have come to expect. She's of Indian origin and speaks with what Patricia – in a less fraught situation – might have described as a white person's Durban accent.

'I'm glad you came. You must be Patricia.'

'Yes.'

'I'm sorry to bring you here. But — there's something I would like to talk to you about.'

Mrs Bell appears on cue from behind her. A tall woman on the far side of fifty with a mop of hair dyed a reddish-brown and eyeliner smeared from weeping. She was John's secretary during all his years as headmaster — and, for all Patricia knows, she works at the school still. John always liked to claim that Mrs Bell could be trusted, but Patricia has never had an actual conversation with her, let alone looked at her properly.

'Hello, Patricia.'

Mrs Bell speaks as though they are better acquainted, almost friends — and inevitably brought closer through this event.

As she returns the greeting, it occurs to Patricia that she doesn't even know Mrs Bell's first name: they always called her Mrs Bell.

'What happened exactly?' she asks.

Mrs Bell inclines her body towards the policewoman, leaving her to speak.

'The case is obviously still under investigation,' the policewoman says, 'but it appears Mr Ford has taken his own life.'

Patricia says nothing to this. She still can't quite believe it: in her head, John would have been the last person to do such a thing. But then what does she know about him — and the contents of his head? They've been having much the same conversation for years now. It rarely touched on anything dangerous in her, so why should it have been any different for him?

'But — I saw him yesterday. He seemed extremely well.'

'So you didn't know?' says Mrs Bell almost enthusiastically. 'He didn't tell you?'

'Tell me what?'

'About the cancer. All the way up his spine. Last week the doctor gave him a couple of months. Apparently it had recently spread to his brain.'

She had not for a moment expected this, of course. She stands there bewildered, feeling caught out — humiliated. She can feel Mrs Bell's gaze on her: it is far too interested to be decent.

'No,' she says, 'I knew nothing about that.'

'Well,' the policewoman says more kindly, 'it seems he left a note about you.'

Patricia sees then that the policewoman is holding a piece of paper, folded in half, with Mrs Bell's name scrawled across it. There was always an extravagance about John's handwriting that used to annoy and somehow belittle her.

'What does it say?'

The policewoman gives her the paper while Mrs Bell looks knowingly on. It reads: *'Dear Janet, please don't disturb Patricia with news of this event. With thanks, John.'*

'Do you know why he would write that?' the policewoman says.

'No,' says Patricia. 'But I imagine he wanted to spare me – at least for a bit.'

'Spare you?' the policewoman continues. 'Spare you what, exactly?'

The opportunity to care – to feel extravagantly?

'I don't know,' Patricia says, 'but he knew I was supposed to be leaving for Durban today. Perhaps he didn't want to stop me.'

'I see,' the policewoman says. 'And the two of you were friends?'

'Old friends. Yes.'

Does Mrs Bell smirk slightly at this, or is Patricia imagining it? What is Mrs Bell – she suddenly wonders – some sort of moralist? She certainly has a sufficient amount of malice.

'Well, I'm sorry. It must come as a terrible shock.'

'Yes.'

The policewoman seems to be waiting for her to say something more, but Patricia has nothing more to say.

'Where is he?' she says, simply in order to speak.

'We've laid him out on the bed. The domestic worker found him in the bathroom. The poor woman thought he'd been murdered. She immediately called the police.'

'Agnes – yes.'

'Would you like to see him?'

Patricia can sense the other two women are expecting her to decline this and hurry away, but Patricia now finds that she actually would like to see him. She would like to look at his face and find out whether or not it is too late to care about him – or feel extravagantly.

'I think I would like to see him – yes.'

Mrs Bell lets out another sniff of what feels like disapproval before moving away. What was it with this woman? Was she outraged or merely jealous? Perhaps she had also been in love with John. Perhaps she had even been his lover. What did Patricia know about John but one or two facts? In other words, nothing at all.

Patricia turns away from the other woman and edges forwards with the walker – as if wanting to signal to Mrs Bell her crippled body, her helplessness in the world. But Mrs Bell is already withdrawing down the corridor, towards the stoep.

'I'm ready,' she says, feeling the long dark pull of John's body from the other room – knowing she'll never be ready for this.

The policewoman nods and moves towards the bedroom – slowly, so as to give the older woman the opportunity to shuffle along. Patricia doesn't look at the watercolours along the corridor that he painted during their years together. The landscapes of nearby places they visited: Caversham Mill, Inverurie Falls, Midmar Dam. For one of his birthdays, she got them all framed together – each one with the same cream mounting and black border. Amongst them are also other landscapes he explored with the boys: mainly the foothills and peaks of the Drakensberg. He claimed to have slept in every cave in the region, the boys cooking their rice and Toppers over their gas stoves, lying on the rocky earth as the rain drummed all night outside – waking to miracles of snow, or waterfalls frozen into a million shards over a precipice.

All of it culminated at the end of this thin corridor, this doomed room – after all that light and open space, after each day of getting up and getting things done, after all his noble words in assembly, on Speech Day, in chapel – this was the nature of John's passing.

But she will think about all of this only later: she is deciding instead that she will have to remain close by him until he's buried, and that they will have to delay their departure for Durban. She recalls again that she never quite believed they would leave the farm. As for Looksmart's estate, it could grow up all around them, and she and Richard could remain in the house, and those who came to live there afterwards could peer at them through the windows like visitors at the aquarium – staring at strange fish from another time.

Only the bedside lamp is on, the soft pool of light cutting across half his face. From a distance, the dear weathered features look intact – and he seems relaxed and solemn at first, the mouth longer, the nose much more prominent, the eyes sunk back into themselves, knowing their job is done. She looks for the wound and finds a dark blot under his chin where the bullet went in. She can't think what has happened to the back of his head. Which is lying deeper into the pillow than might have been expected. It is too horrendous to contemplate: her mind gawps at it. Instead, she looks at his downturned mouth that once – in another life – she kissed. It was a mouth, she once told him, that always looked rather dismayed in sleep.

She is used to seeing the dead: the life leaked out of them, so that all that remains is the vessel, its bloodless glow. She has seen expressions of agony and calm, optimism and dread, fixed in time – and always death's equanimity shining through. There was only ever a distant kinship between the dead body and the one that had lived, which always suggested to her that the body was not the point after all, and that it only acquired its true status in death, having claimed far too much importance for itself during life.

She can hardly remember her mother dead. The new vacancy running through the house like a dry wind is what she remembers most of all, not the body itself. And what she recalls most about the body of her father was its smallness: not only the length of him but the narrowness of his shoulders, the neatness of his limbs, the fine bony child's hands, the head not much bigger than a doll's. Was this all there was to him? she remembers thinking. He looked like he could have been folded up and fitted into one of his desk drawers.

What sets the body of John aside is the violence of his death – the violence he has done to himself. She can't look at him and not think of it, not wonder at it. He is two things now: John dead and a man who found it in himself to end his life. This first man she can still approach with her intuition, her thought. She can find John's calm in him, his solitude. This man looks much the same size as she remembers him, and his hands are still recognisable to her – and turned almost outwards, as if inviting her to take hold of them. But that other man – the one who killed himself – that man is pushing the more familiar man aside, insisting on the mystery that must run through all things.

Patricia can sense the policewoman at the door, looking and not looking, neither in the room nor out of it. For a moment, she confuses the woman with herself, and feels that she – Patricia – no longer exists where she exists. And so she gasps air into her, and as she does so she imagines that the other woman is mistaking this sound for grief. But it isn't grief: she's still far too dislocated to feel anything so coherent yet.

She looks at the face for the last time and sees he must have shaved shortly before his death. There's a bit of shaving cream below his earlobe and a brief crop of hairs under his chin that was left out. She wonders what this man thought as he shaved himself in the small round mirror above the sink. Whether he knew he was going to kill himself. Whether he still believed in God. Or did he find – when it came down to it – that he could put aside the idea of God as easily as he could put aside the idea of his own life?

'What happens now?' she says.

'He'll be taken to the forensics laboratory in 'Maritzburg. Mrs Bell has informed his next of kin.'

'I'm sure she has.'

As the policewoman carries on speaking, she finds she doesn't want to see John's children. Or watch them crowding around his coffin – with their Australian spouses and their Australian children – pretending his passing is a huge loss to them – while all the time eyeing the grandfather clock in the hallway, the antique officer's sword above the fireplace and the dining room table. They will no doubt want to argue over the paintings along the corridor – whose meaning only she can explain – and will wonder who that lingering overweight woman is, with her perplexed expression and whiff of sour cream.

'Goodbye, John,' she says.

But John only answers back with his silence: the hard knot of vacancy that will now be in the world whenever she turns to him. She leans forward slightly and breathes in the smell of him. There is only a trace of his tobacco and his cologne. Stronger than this, and growing stronger, is the smell of a butchery, of something recently butchered.

As she leaves the house – the walker clanking patiently – she sees his pipe sitting on the table by the door, along with a bowl of dying lemon-coloured roses and a tube of half-used Super Glue. Mrs Bell is waiting for her outside, perched on the bonnet of her yellow car, smoking a cigarette. Everything looks impossibly bright and out of joint, and Mrs Bell – who can move far faster – approaches her with an apparent appetite to talk, to gather information about Patricia's reactions, perhaps to hurt Patricia with fresh revelations.

But it's all too much, and before the other woman can get a word in, Patricia says: 'I'll be leaving for Durban now, Janet. I'm sorry I won't be able to return for the funeral.'

Mrs Bell is stopped in her tracks, perhaps stunned into submission by the violence in her voice, or the note of what sounds like blame. In order to soften this, Patricia adds: 'I'm sure the last thing his children will need is me hanging about.'

'Of course,' says Mrs Bell, bright and sharp – deciding, perhaps, that Patricia is not such a worthy opponent after all.

John

My dear Patricia

It is late at night as I write this. The wind is in the trees. An eagle-owl is hooting. A motorbike winds away down some country road — and I think of the driver, a young man probably, living in a world I would barely recognise.

Who are we? What will we leave behind us when we go? I will have a cricket field named after me. A few anecdotes — most of them unpleasant. And two children who live in another time zone who usually try to avoid my calls on a Sunday night.

As I write this, I imagine you in Durban already, sitting in your room with its window to the sea — these pages in your lap. Since I first met you, you have talked about that house, that room, and how you will one day return to it. Well, now that you're there, I hope you'll get some of the peace you've been longing for.

We are reaching the end of our days, dear friend — and I find I've done much to be ashamed of. I think I lacked the patience to be a husband, a father, a headmaster, as I lacked the patience to care properly for my dying wife. I wonder where my anger came from. The heavens? My blood? The impotence we must all feel when we sit alone in a house at night — as I am — and look back at the mess we've made of our lives?

I have no idea what I'm trying to say. These days my mind gets all muddled the minute I turn towards it. I suppose I wanted to thank you for loving me, for not giving up on me. Although our love was wrong in the eyes of the world, our time together is one of the things I don't regret — on the contrary, it was a place of truth, a place that allowed me to breathe again and remind myself of the man I might have become.

I hope you'll forgive my shortcomings and remember some of our happy times. Like our room at the hotel that overlooked the lake — and that afternoon when the snow arrived and we stood at the window in our underwear, knowing that for a while at least we would be free.

Be brave, my love, and know that I will be ahead of you. I hope to meet you over a cup of coffee, a song on the radio, or between the lines of a good book.

Think well of us — and of each of us.

Yours
John

Patricia

Bheki is fitting the suitcases together in the boot of the car. The blue trunk
went in first and everything else – including the walker – is being arranged
around it. In another part of the garden, Richard is inspecting the roses.
Sometimes he turns around and looks behind him, as if expecting Rupert
and George still to be nosing about somewhere at his heels. It's an innocuous-looking scene: the silver air thinning around them, the promise of sun-
shine. They look like any other family about to set off on holiday.

John's letter is the closest she has ever got to receiving a love letter from
anyone. She was moved on her first reading of it, when she took it at its word
– but when she read it again and tried to understand it, she was plagued with
such a range of conflicting thoughts that she could hardly carry on reading.
The letter was no doubt written with the knowledge that he had cancer and
was planning to kill himself. He most likely imagined she would have learned
these two facts by the time she got to Durban and finally read it. So he wanted

her to think he was sparing her, being considerate. But this is exactly what irks her: at the moment of writing, when he could have confessed to anything at all without fear of contradiction, he chose to withhold himself – just as he withheld that goblet of wine he liked to carry around with him at church.

The one thing she hadn't provided for John was a place of truth. The truth had eluded him. It had eluded both of them. Never before has she felt further from him than now – after reading his well-intentioned letter. She couldn't help but see the letter for what it really was: as wishful thinking, as a piece of sentimentality dredged up in the dead of night. Nowhere did he ever say he loved her: even at the far end of the world, surrounded by an infinity of darkness, this hadn't been his style.

The letter is still in her lap when Beauty appears at the doorway and finds her sitting on the wheelchair on the stoep. Behind them stands the house, a place that will forget them within a few days of their departure: the trace of them in the remaining boxes, and then the smell of them – until the house exists as a cave does, but without their names carved into the walls.

But Beauty seems barely conscious of the house. Her look is far away. It is the expression of someone watching a figure coming towards them from a distance – a figure that is coming to invade their peace.

'Are we ready?' Patricia says, turning in the wheelchair.

Beauty shrugs in a way that suggests they will never be ready: now is as good a moment to leave as any.

'All these years,' Patricia says, 'and you never said a word.'

Beauty does not turn and look at her. She seems to be pretending that she has not heard Patricia's words. But Patricia can see that the woman has heard her from the slight hardness in her gaze.

Patricia tries to smile at her.

'Come,' she says. 'Talk to me.'

She gestures towards a wicker chair – its legs frayed by the claws of a long-departed cat – and invites Beauty to sit. After a moment, Beauty complies – but with her feet still on the ground, so that in an instant she might dart off.

'Why didn't you leave?'

'When, Mesis?'

'When you were old enough. You could have gone anywhere.'

'But Mesis – this is where I live.'

Ethunzini stirs nearby in her basket, sensing the irregularity of all this. Out in the garden, her grave is waiting, nothing more than a simple hole in the ground – the kind that might be used to plant a tree. But neither of the women notices the dog or is thinking about her. Their heads are drawn together, as if the one is humming a tune the other is trying to remember.

'Why did you stay silent?'

'This job, it was good for me.'

'Was it really?'

'And my family – they have always lived here.'

They are speaking so quietly that it would be difficult to hear them from a few paces off, even though there is no need for such secrecy. Richard is still out in the garden, being prompted along by a phantom bee, and Bheki is having to repack the boot from scratch because – try as he might – he still can't get it shut.

'But aren't you angry?'

Beauty looks at Patricia with apparent incomprehension. Not because she doesn't understand the question but more because she doesn't understand why Patricia should ask it, or want to encourage it.

'Mesis?'

'Aren't you angry – about what happened to Grace?'

'I was a child, Mesis. I didn't know if I should be angry.'

Patricia stares hard at the other woman, waiting for her to continue, not wanting to let her slip away with a few words, or a look.

'We do not talk about sis' Grace,' Beauty says. 'When we think of her, we think of her as something – lost.'

'Lost?'

All the years between them have culminated in this moment. The air around them is dim, shutting out the sound of the weavers in the trees, the earthmovers, Bheki's struggle with the suitcases.

'Beauty – please. You have to tell me the truth.'

'But why, Mesis?'

Beauty asks the question genuinely, perhaps wanting to understand what the truth might sound like, or what it might do.

'Because that's all we have left.'

Beauty lets out a sigh that is both grief and impatience.

'Mesis, you really want to know?'

'Yes!'

This word brings Richard to a stop in the garden. He glances in their direction before returning to his pantomime in the garden – sniffing the roses like he has never smelt a rose before.

'I think another day will be better.'

'No – now – today.'

Bheki has almost finished packing the car when he sees Beauty's red suitcase sitting near the passenger door. He goes over and picks it up and returns to the renewed puzzle of the boot.

'Sis' Grace –'

'What? Please, Beauty – we don't have any time!'

'She was with uBaas – there were other times before.'

Neither of them looks up at Richard when Beauty says this, as though the man in the garden is someone else – and the present is far away, no more than a trick of the light.

'What do you mean, exactly?'

Beauty leans forward, her knee knocking the wheel of the wheelchair, making it creak. When she speaks, she does so rapidly, as if each of the words has already been arranged inside her.

'UBaas – he would pay her money each and every time. They said that sis' Grace never loved Looksmart. Not like Looksmart loved her. He was too young for her. His head was –'

'Yes?'

'His head had too much words inside it.'

She says this as if words were no more than rocks, numb and burdensome.

'Sis' Grace said to my mother – she was not wanting to marry him.'

Patricia remembers the two red lights from the night before. Looksmart's satisfied departure. It seems so sad now: the gaps that Looksmart carried away inside him, not even knowing that they were there.

'But he said they loved each other desperately,' she says. 'He said she was good.'

'Good?'

The word hangs in the air like the word 'truth': simply as another way of presenting oneself to the world.

'She had nothing,' Beauty continues, 'and uBaas — he paid her. Sis' Grace did not think about good or not good. Ubezama ukuphila.'

'She was trying to survive?'

Patricia has to repeat the phrase in English in order to accept it fully.

'When sis' Grace died, she was pregnant with uBaas's child.'

'She was pregnant with Richard's child?'

'Yebo, Mesis.'

Bheki has finally managed to arrange the luggage so that he can close the boot — which he now does, gingerly. He looks like a man going through the very last gestures of respect.

'What about Richard. Did he know?'

Beauty leans in closer and speaks with absolute urgency and clarity, like one of those men whispering advice into the mind of a boxer as he is about to re-enter the ring.

'Before she died, sis' Grace told him. It was at the dairy, in that room they went to, where the milk tank is. He was angry because she wanted to keep it, the child. She told him it went against her customs, her religion, to kill a child. I heard it from outside the door, listening. Then he started to swear, he hit her and I came inside. She ran away screaming, screaming about the child — and uBaas, he came to the road and he freed his dog on her.'

'My — God.'

Beauty is watching her, trying to see how much more she can take. What else could there be? What else to take?

'Why didn't you tell Looksmart about this yesterday?'

'Looksmart is like a boy. In his heart. He will not be able to hear a thing like that.'

Bheki is standing at the car, looking across at them. In his hand, he holds the shotgun Patricia inherited from her father, but neither she nor Beauty acknowledges him.

'Looksmart has his own story,' Patricia says. 'He was very — convincing about it. Why must I now believe you?'

Beauty straightens up. She looks across at Bheki and seems to consider the gun. When she speaks, it's as if the conversation is already concluded – and she will have no further part in it.

'Mesis,' she says, 'you must find the truth for yourself.'

They don't speak for a while. Bheki stands there with the gun and Richard paces the garden, a slight springiness in his step that means he is needing to pee. It still feels to Patricia that the man in the garden is someone else: little more than a photograph of a relative already long dead.

There was no name for it. That was what Richard said last night. Two dead children. I have two dead children for the ambulance to pick up. Didn't he say something like that?

'He killed his own child,' she says.

'For uBaas – there was no child.'

Patricia shakes her head. She knows that Beauty is wrong, that Richard felt more about that child than he could ever have admitted, but she doesn't say this: there's no longer any point in trying to defend him.

'When we go to Durban, I will put him in a home.'

Beauty looks at her with apparent incomprehension and a fresh note of indifference regarding Richard's fate.

'A home?' she says.

'A home that is for people who are sick.'

Bheki

He does not know what they are saying, the Madam and Beauty, but he is not so interested in that. They are forever talking between themselves, those two, like conspiring children. But when Beauty moves away to fetch the Baas, he approaches the Madam with her father's gun. It feels for a moment like he might shoot her — and although the Madam is too far away to sense this, apparently the dog does: it growls at him from its basket. It does not understand that it should not be protecting the Madam: it should be protecting itself.

'I'm sorry to ask you to do it, Bheki,' she says.

Which is her way of asking him to do it.

But he doesn't mind killing the dog. He killed the other two without a thought. It is not that he is a hard man, but he has his own ideas of justice.

'You'll have to do it where she sits,' the Madam says.

They both know that if he tries to move the dog, it will want to bite him.

There will be a bigger mess. It will be easier if he kills the dog in the comfort of her basket. Afterwards he can use the hosepipe to clean everything up.

As he approaches, the dog continues its growling – a low gravelly sound that is closer to a lament. The Madam has moved her wheelchair away, as expected, but Bheki finds he can look straight into the dog's eyes without a problem. The dog knows that something is wrong. Its gaze alternates between the Madam and Bheki, but it finds that its support is not there where expected: the Madam has turned her back on it. And yet, deep down, Bheki can see that the dog trusts her still: it gulps, putting on a brave face, and licks its chops, perhaps hoping Bheki will hand it a biscuit or a bone. The dog does not understand how much the world has changed. It still believes that a man like Bheki will always come second to a dog, and that such a man will never be allowed to harm it.

Richard

At the sound of the shot, he looks up from his rose. The sweet wet smell of it still sings somewhere at the back of his head, reminding him of summers in England a long time ago. A park and a slippery dark green fountain, a brass band playing in dappled light under a copper beech, a blue balloon he let go that almost immediately disappeared into the blueness of sky. He doesn't know what all the fuss is about. The long black man is lifting a heavy sack of what looks like dog and is carrying it across the grass and the old woman in the wheelchair lets a piece of paper fly off from her hand – and for a moment he's tempted to go over there and get to the bottom of all this, but instead he's drawn back to the pale peach colour of the rose, which grows in intensity very quietly towards the centre and has tiny insects crawling in and out of it – long and pale brown, and with no name he has ever known.

Patricia

The sun is shining through the cloud when she climbs into the car, as if things are finally looking up on the farm now that they're leaving it. Bheki starts up the engine and they sit for a while, considering, before he puts the car into gear and it begins to roll forward over the uneven lawn. On the stoep is Ethunzini's vacant basket – with a puddle of water drying around it.

'Did you lock the front door?'

'Yebo, Madam.'

'And the wheelchair?'

'It is inside.'

'Well – I should probably buy a new one in Durban. That one's started to dig into my back.'

Without commenting on this, Bheki takes the keys from his pocket and hands them to her. They are still warm from the warmth of him. She knows every key on this bunch and is familiar with every lock: she knows exactly how to manipulate every lock, because some of them are old and difficult, and someone who didn't know them might think at first that the key didn't fit. Not knowing what else to do with them, Patricia puts the keys in the cubbyhole amongst her papers. The other set of keys is with the removal men, who will let themselves into the house later in the week. She realises then that John's letter is still somewhere on the stoep, but she decides to leave it there, for the paper itself is hardly the point.

She can see the bloodwoods – tall and wet and winking in the sunlight – but otherwise there are to be no witnesses to their departure. Richard and Beauty are sitting in the back, as far apart as possible, turned slightly away from each other. Patricia can see Beauty's blank stare in the rear-view mirror, but Richard is almost entirely out of sight. She can only hear him humming to himself, as is his habit these days, the sound so discreet it is almost below hearing.

'The rain is finished.'

Bheki says this as if he is speaking not of the rain but of a broader event – a war or a plague. Patricia wonders what Bheki knows about all that has passed between herself, Beauty and Looksmart, and she wonders what he might think about it. But she also senses that the events of that day will never be spoken of again – not if anyone can help it. Even if that double beast in the garden will always be circling somewhere near the centre of their lives, dripping blood.

'Yes,' she says, 'isn't it going to be a lovely day?'

She intends this as an ironic statement, but it doesn't come out that way: it bristles with a range of meanings, some of them good.

They pass the long ruin of the stables, the rubble steaming in the morning light, the fresh crop of weeds already carrying a few yellow butterflies. The first of the builders – each of them in florescent jackets – are trooping away across a field to one of the half-built houses. The emerging sky is so blue that it looks almost mauve through Patricia's window, and when she looks in it for birds she's pleased to discover a single swallow darting back and forth, like a tadpole bumping around inside a fishbowl, looking for a place to get out.

She wants to say goodbye to the farm, to wish it well, but this would sound foolish in front of her companions. She suspects that they are feeling sorry for her, but when she glances again at their faces they seem lost in their own thoughts – and possibly content. Now that they are leaving the farm, it is no longer hers or Richard's, but simply a place where each of them has lived.

They are about to reach the marsh when they see another car coming towards them. It is being driven with a certain gentility, attempting to avoid every runnel and rock. No one in the car says anything, but when they are near enough to see the driver's face, Bheki pulls over to one side, the large Mercedes ascending the thick grass, quite accustomed to such a manoeuvre on this road.

Looksmart's car window glides down in half the time it takes Bheki to lower his window – for not only is Bheki's mechanism old and stiff but the plastic knob was long ago gnawed off by one of the dogs.

'Hello,' Looksmart says.

He looks a bit embarrassed and it's clear that he was hoping they had left. Today he is wearing a navy blue golfing shirt and he looks affluent and comfortable. Patricia suspects that she misjudged him yesterday: he was probably far more at home in that suit than she gave him credit for.

'Are you coming to make sure we're actually leaving?' she jokes.

He doesn't seem to hear her properly and says, 'I'm sorry, I didn't mean – I thought you'd be gone.'

She and Looksmart try to see each other past the other heads and through the gloom of the cars, but they remain little more to one another than a silhouette.

'I suppose he'll be wanting the keys,' she says to Bheki.

She takes the keys out of the cubbyhole and Bheki lobs them through the air to Looksmart, who catches them easily. There is an opportunity for one of them to speak, to say a few words that might help them to laugh the moment away, but each of them keeps their peace – and as the two drivers ease forward, they raise their hands and carry on.

Acknowledgements

I would like to thank Terry Morris, Andrea Nattrass, Laura Hammond and all at Picador Africa for their continued support. Thanks also to all those who have contributed towards the growth of this novel: especially Michael Titlestad and Alison Lowry for their rigour and care. For the isiZulu translations I am indebted to Jacob Ntshangase and Babongile Zulu. Much thanks also to André Brink, Mark Behr, Michele Magwood and Nadine Gordimer for their endorsements. In the last months of her life, and in spite of her illness, Nadine Gordimer still managed to find the time to read the manuscript and offer words of encouragement. Thank you also to my beautiful, magical wife Leila, and to my daughter Phoebe, who did an excellent job of dragging me away from the manuscript – and back to the world of splinters, princess plasters and bicycle rides through the park.

About the author

Craig Higginson is an internationally renowned, multi-award-winning play-wright and novelist who lives in Johannesburg. His previous novels include *The Hill* (Jacana), and *Last Summer* and *The Landscape Painter* (both Picador Africa). His plays include *Dream of the Dog, The Girl in the Yellow Dress, The Jungle Book, Little Foot* and *The Imagined Land* (all published by Oberon Books, London). At present Craig is working on two new plays, *The Red Door* and *The Mission Song* (the second an adaptation of John le Carre's novel for Headlong [London] and John le Carre's production company The Ink Factory [London and Los Angeles]), as well as a new novel set in Paris – intended for release in 2017. *The Dream House* will be the first of his novels to appear in French in 2016 (Mercure de France); *Last Summer* will follow in 2017.

Printed by BoD™in Norderstedt, Germany